A Caledo
Col'ecti

A Compilation of Short Stories

Edited by David Field

Library and Archives Canada Cataloguing in Publication

A Caledon collection / edited by David Field.

ISBN 978-0-9738221-9-9

     1. Short stories, Canadian (English)--Ontario--Caledon.
2. Canadian fiction (English)--21st century.
I. Field, David, 1980-

PS8329.7.C32C28 2009   C813'.01089713535   C2009-906172-4

Printed and bound in Canada.
Cover photograph: Paul Forster
Cover and book design: David Field

Published by
Giant Beaver Publications
32 Stadium Road
Suite 329
Toronto, Ontario M5V 3P4
Telephone: 1-866-844-6675

Visit Giant Beaver Publications' website: www.giantbeaver.com

Table of Contents

(By Story)

Table of Contents
(By Author)

Introduction

David Field

Creating a collection of short stories like this one takes many people and lots of time. This book was born after 11 short stories were chosen from the original 42 submissions. The amount of stories submitted was astonishing and it took the work of a hard working panel to read every single one of them and a good many hours discussing which stories should be included in the book. A collection of ten stories would have been a nice round number, but it is not always easy to choose, and we just could not reduce the book by one more story. Thank you to Paul Forster, Donna Kamiel-Forster, Ray Manninen, Kelley Potter, and Mary Maw for all their work in selecting the stories for this collection.

Every author in this book deserves a huge thank you. It has been a pleasure working with you. Thank you for letting me read your story, make constructive criticism, and for producing even better stories than were originally submitted for consideration. Your hard work and patience have resulted in a fantastic collection that you should be proud of. You all are the stars of this book.

A very special thanks is due to Paul Forster and Donna Kamiel-Forster who conceived this book and coordinated everything. Without them this book would never have gotten the start it needed. At the conclusion of this project, Paul Forster, Donna Kamiel-Forster, Ray Manninen, Kelly Potter and Tasha Potter helped by giving everything a final proofread.

From the point a book is conceived it takes on a life of its own. What a life this book has had. I know its publication is just the beginning. Thank you for supporting this book and helping its life to flourish.

Shackles of Tradition

Raisa Austina Palha

Sholak trudged beneath the weight that made him stoop. It was a goat's carcass in a camel-skin bag; he carried it unsteadily. He walked amidst the sand dunes, his weather-beaten sandals drawing up clouds of sand with every step. A musty handkerchief on his shoulder, he continually swiped beads of perspiration that travelled down his forehead with his hand. His skin felt caked and gritty, a mixture of perspiration and sand.

It was with the usual nomadic spirit that his clan, the Hayy tribe of the Bedouin people, had awoken this morning. The sun had risen in the East; a new day had begun. After relishing a breakfast of oat cereal, dates, and milk, the tribe hoisted all its belongings onto camels, forming caravans, ready to move on in its journey—a perpetual quest for more fertile pastures. Drought had stolen every drop of moisture in the old land, compelling them to journey east, to greener ground.

Ahead of Sholak, the rest of his tribal family moved along. The blazing heat beat down on them. In the distance, the horizon seemed a resplendent ocean, little luminous waves. But Sholak wasn't fooled. What was once, to him, an unreachable expanse of water was now a mere optical illusion. What was once a confounding physical mystery was now a sure-footed fact, backed by scientific investigation, rationalized in the texts of Uncle Taru. Sholak stopped to adjust his baggage. He looked ahead. Guiding the camels onward, at the front of the tribe, was his father, Sheikh Hamad, the Hayy tribe leader. Even through his long white robe, Sholak could see the well-defined physique of a warrior, akin to those of the generation who had gone before. Sholak marvelled at his father's athletic form. Next to him, Sholak looked like a frail reed of barley.

As he trod on in silence, Sholak prayed that the rage that had consumed his father the night just past was extinguished. Before the journey out of the old land, Sholak had stolen into a tent to get another glimpse at a Western magazine (one of many) that his Uncle Taru had loaned to him. His eyes had absorbed as much of the mystique of the West as they could, but Sholak was never quite satisfied. Once again, he scanned the glossy pages of Life magazine, with its photographs of fast automobiles with glistening wheels, of rugged men puffing on Marlboros and Camels, of awesome skyscrapers that kissed the sky.

So engrossed was he in this other worldly utopia that he did not sense his father's presence behind him. Sheikh Hamad loomed over Sholak. He stood for a while watching his son resting on his stomach, flipping through the magazine. In a rage and without warning, he pressed his weather-beaten sandal onto his son's back, crushing him with the weight of his foot. Sholak yelped and shielded his head with his hands, anticipating a blow to his head. His body grew numb with fear. He hid his face in shame, avoiding his father's glare. Sheikh Hamad snatched the magazine off the floor.

"You filthy rascal! Abominable fool!" Sheikh Hamad shouted, digging deeper into Sholak's back with his dirty foot. "I'm sure your Uncle Taru is to blame for this! Filling your mind with such rot! Are you that corruptible? Have you not the least bit of consideration for our tradition? I forbid you to ever see him again!"

Sholak heard the rip of paper. From the corner of his eye he saw shreds of the magazine falling to the floor. "Get the camels ready for our journey tomorrow," Sheikh Hamad said, seething.

He gave his son a final kick in his side and left him wriggling like a worm.

Thinking about the incident of the previous night, Sholak's knees trembled. He capitulated to the ground. Lately, he was feeling a great heaviness in his heart. He had once believed nomadic spirit—nomadic blood—as infused into him, an integral part of himself. That was in the days of his tender youth, when there was no knowing otherwise, no alternative perspective on life. Now, with the coming of adolescence, he felt a certain yearning to be alone—a free and independent man, liberated from the shackles of tradition. Tradition would destine him to become leader of the tribe once his father passed on to the next life. With no one else to inherit the title, Sholak would have to shoulder that responsibility. His mind reeled at the prospect. He would make an unfit leader.

Sholak picked up his load and carried it unsteadily. Nightfall was nearing and the tribe had finally reached the village of Sabu, its destination. It slowed its pace as it entered. Mud huts could be seen in the distance. Surrounding them was a vast expanse of land: fertile plains suitable for growing rice, wheat, and barley.

But Sholak noted a change in the landscape. In the far distance tall buildings loomed—unfamiliar greys in a foreground of green. Was he imagining this scene? He closed his eyes and reopened them. This was no illusion. His land was morphing into a concrete jungle—like the one he had seen in Life magazine. The world of the West was encroaching onto his land.

Sholak let down his load with a great thump. The aroma of congealed blood and rancid flesh penetrated the air and assailed his nostrils. He retched. A little way ahead, Sheikh Hamad alighted from his camel.

"We will be staying in the village for the duration of summertime. Come winter, we will go back into the desert," he declared.

After the tribe was given instructions, it scattered. Head-stooped and timid, Sholak followed Sheikh Hamad and helped set up their tent. He spoke not a word lest he aggravate his father.

* * *

Sholak arose with the sun. He stretched and breathed the cool morning air, allowing it to revitalize him. He looked about the tent, searching for his father—he was not to be found. *Yes! He has left to finish business in the village.* Sholak was at liberty to do whatever he pleased—until evening anyway. He quickly took a refreshing bath, dressed, and started on his visit to Uncle Taru's.

Uncle Taru was known as a reformist. Recruited by the government as a policeman in the city of Azarbaar, he threatened the Hayy tribe's sense of tradition and unity. No one ever forgot how, years ago, he had left the nomads in pursuit of a more modern existence.

To the tribe, Uncle Taru was a heedless old fool: abandoning tradition for modernity, escaping the conventional lifestyle and entering into a world of uncertainty. But to Sholak, the man was a dear friend and role model—courageous, kind, and loving, a stark contrast to his brother, the fierce and adamant Sheikh Hamad.

Sholak took the bus from the periphery of Azarbaar to his uncle's house in the heart of the city. Uncle Taru's house was modern: it was modestly spacious, made of brick, with a well-tended garden in the backyard. Sholak rapped the doorknocker and waited.

A figure eventually appeared. Dressed in a flowing white robe, fresh-faced, and smiling, Uncle Taru opened the door.

"*Assalam alaikum*," Taru greeted his nephew.

"*Wa'alaikum assalam*," Sholak replied.

Uncle Taru motioned toward a luxurious sofa in his living room. "You've made it safely, my loving child! I'm so happy to see you here again." They embraced. "Come in, come in! What are you standing outside for?"

"So how was the journey here? Tough?" Uncle Taru called from the kitchen. No doubt he was preparing some of his delicious kiwi fruit drink. Sholak licked his lips.

"Yes. We travelled for miles. The journey seemed endless—as always," Sholak responded. "Droughts in the Hiraar region compelled us to move. Hopefully we will stay in the village for a long time. I hate moving about so much."

"Then why move? Settle down, my child," Uncle Taru said,

emerging from the kitchen. He held in his hand a glass of Sholak's favourite beverage. Sholak took it politely, thanking him. His uncle continued, "How old are you? Almost twenty? You know, Sholak, truly there is something wonderful out there in the wider world. But to learn what that is, you have to come out of your shell, your safety net, your circle of friends and family."

"I'm not like you, Uncle. I'm not at all brave. I don't think I have it in me," Sholak replied despondently.

"Do not give me that nonsense! Of course you do! I see it in your eyes—that adventurer's spirit. Years of your father's tyranny have not managed to subdue it. You want to explore the world for yourself and become much more than who you are now."

"You sense correctly, Uncle. But—you know father. Ever since mother, peace be upon her, left this world, he has developed a heart of stone. It's hard for me to talk to him about anything these days. If I did gather enough courage to speak with him about finally settling down, I fear about the plan not working. Besides, father—he'd be furious!" Sholak said. There was no use. He was a coward, a slave to tradition.

"Change requires courage," Uncle Taru said. "Government has uprooted the livelihood of many tribal people, offering them new opportunities, more land, and a better way of living. I always wondered what life would be like if I was to abandon the nomadic way of life—the aimless journey to nowhere. Initially, I was afraid, but when I got out, I loved everything about my new life. I still do. No regrets whatsoever. If changes are taking place for the better, then why don't people seize them?"

"How rapidly things are changing!" Sholak exclaimed. "While coming here I saw all the new buildings that have been constructed. There weren't so many when I was here last."

"Yes, my boy. There's been rapid progress," Uncle Taru said. "Listen, an opportunity has made itself available. I have a friend who owns a hotel in the city and he is looking for a linen-porter. He wants someone responsible and hard-working. I immediately thought of you."

"But father would—" Sholak started.

"You never know, son. You could start off small and maybe work up to be the manager of the place. I have faith in you. Tell me you will consider it."

"I will consider it," Sholak said meekly.

"Good," Uncle Taru said. He grinned at Sholak. "Now, look what I have for you!" He dodged behind the sofa he was sitting on and pulled out the latest issue of Life magazine. On the front cover was a picture of pop sensation Michael Jackson.

"The King of Pop," Uncle Taru said. "In the back room of the hotel, one of the workers, Salim, plays his music. He'll play the same song about ten, maybe twenty, times. Drives me crazy, that fool!" He laughed.

Sholak eyed the magazine nervously. He wondered whether or not to tell his uncle about what had happened last night—he quickly decided against it. Talking about his father any more would kill their good mood.

"Thank you, Uncle," Sholak said, taking the magazine and hugging it to his chest.

Uncle Taru and Sholak talked for hours. When evening drew close and the sun was descending on the horizon, Sholak got up with a start. "Uncle, I have to go! Father will be home any minute!"

"Take care, my child. Hope to see you soon," Uncle Taru said.

Sholak embraced his uncle hurriedly and ran to catch the next bus. His mind teemed with a thousand thoughts.

✳ ✳ ✳

Sheikh Hamad paced impatiently outside his tent. A tremendous rage pulsed through his veins. It took the form of words when the nimble figure of his son approached him. Sholak froze dead in his tracks upon seeing the paternal rage.

Sheikh Hamad demanded. "Where were you all this time? The sun has set. " His gaze travelled to the magazine in his son's hands. "Taru! I told you to stay away from him! Didn't I tell you to stay away from him?"

Sholak didn't respond immediately. His gaze travelled to the line of tents ahead of him. The caravan had scattered and the camels lay about in torpor. A slight breeze ruffled the canvas of the tents. The scene brought to Sholak's mind a picture he had once seen in a Western magazine called National Geographic. He could not read the article, which was in English, but from the pictures he gleaned that the West was making a mockery of his culture. Look at these barbarians, these backward heathens, and their quaint ways, the pictures seemed to say. Sholak did not want to be entertainment for the Western world. He turned his gaze back to his father.

"Answer me!" Sheikh Hamad cried, spittle flying out of his mouth. He penetrated Sholak's eyes with his glare.

Sholak simmered silently. For years he had put up a silent forbearance, bearing the abuse of his father. He had suffered his angst and humiliation privately, like a stoic. But every human being has a threshold beyond which it will not endure injustice. Sholak had arrived at that moment. Rage sweltered in him also, pounding to be let out.

"I'm almost twenty. Do you think I am happy?" Sholak began quietly, through gritted teeth. "No. I am not. There are many things I want to do but you are stopping me from doing them. I want to be somebody. I want an identity. I want to go places, meet people. It's the twentieth century, father. Open your eyes. Things have changed. The whole world is moving forward. Except us. Open your eyes."

Sheikh Hamad was astounded by his son's boldness. He stood dumbstruck for seconds. Then, with long strides he approached Sholak, his right arm in mid-air.

Sholak ducked the first blow. After barely dodging the second one, he ran past his father. He ran till his lungs pounded and he couldn't run anymore. He headed for the outskirts of the village. His mind was racing. *I'll seize the position of linen-porter at the hotel Uncle Taru told me about. The salary might be enough to sustain me.* Yes, that's what he would do. He had come to a decision. Finally. He would make the leap, from primitivism to modernity. He would break the shackles of tradition.

Father would be enraged. But Sholak would come back after he had created a new life for himself. Only then. The breeze blew through his hair as he ran to the bus stop. Sometimes one just has to escape. For the first time in his life he felt incredibly light and free. It was exhilarating. He sped on faster.

Moebius

Stephen David Wilsher

W hat are those little squares called that are there when you don't look at them but as soon as you do disappear, the ones that are formed at the intersection of crossing lines? It was just like that: I was standing under the street lamp where River Street and Greenwich Avenue meet, at two o'clock in the morning, one of those mild nights in May, quite pleasant really, with mist in the air, that you could see beneath the halo of the overhead light.

And then it was almost as if someone had whispered quite close in my ear—or called me at a distance from over the hill across the meadow—was it my name—and I swore I saw a light just at the corner of McMurtry's store, or at least I thought I did. When I went to investigate nothing was there, and then I heard the wind in the trees and thought I heard the whisper of my name again. But just then a truck came trundling past, echoing down the corridors of the night-enshrouded town, and the reverie passed.

The next day I was drawn to McMurtry's store to see what I might find. There was nothing of course, but I shivered when I passed the corner where I thought I saw the light. I went in to get a Coke and a Hershey's and waited until Ed was finished with Mrs. Laughton. Ed was the young store manager that McMurtry had hired just last summer. He was new in town, but not so new anymore, and he seemed to be getting on quite well, both as manager of McMurtry's General Goods and as a new citizen to our small town. When Mrs. Laughton left and I heard the jangle of the bells that announced the opening and closing of the front door, the familiar sound that was always somehow so comforting to me, I proceeded to buy the Coke and the chocolate bar, but also to ask Edward Blackstone if he had seen or heard of anything unusual that had happened last night at the corner of Greenwich and River. Ed lived above the store. Of course, he said no, "Not that I know of." What else was he going to say?

Either nothing really had happened and I was imagining things or, if it had, perhaps he had just not seen it. There was of course another possibility: he was still relatively new and settling in; he's not going to start making people think he's crazy. So I left the store with Coke in hand, chocolate bar in my jacket pocket, and an unsettling feeling in my gut and at the nape of my neck that told me that I really had seen something but also that there really wasn't anything that I could do about it. And even if there was, like Ed, I wasn't overly anxious to encourage people to think that I was "out of sorts," so to speak.

I turned down River and walked the mile and a half to the craggy old willow whose roots overhung Miller's Creek, the willow I had practically grown-up with, the one I sometimes liked to go to, to sit under, or when I was younger, to climb up and sit in, to mull things over. It was one of my favourite spots in town, at the edge of the creek where the tree stood alone, far enough out so as to have some privacy, and yet still close enough to the centre of town to be able to get to anywhere I might need to be.

Further away from town was a stand of about twenty black willows, not as old as the craggy old gentleman who was my closer intimate, the black willows which nonetheless I also liked to frequent, where sometimes at twilight you could see fireflies flicking on and off. With fireflies you could actually look at them as they lit and then disappeared, and then lit again. What I had seen and heard near McMurtry's—and I was becoming inexplicably more and more convinced of it all the time—was very different than fireflies, less real and more so. The black willow stand was another two and a half miles along the creek and right then I had a very strong impulse to go there. The trees followed a smaller tributary that emptied into Miller's Creek and beyond it was the marsh where the ground was lower than the surrounding rise, which made it wetter and softer to walk on. But I knew certain places where it was safe to tread, not exactly dry but secure enough to ensure passage.

When I got there, the air was filled with myriad fireflies doing their strobe light dance beneath the trees, and I could see also in the marsh beyond. Five trees away from the junction of the tributary and Miller's Creek was the small wooden bridge over which I crossed to the other side. Soon I was carefully threading my way through the marsh upon the secret spots that let me pass, the air fragrant with its musky aroma. Occasionally, out of the corner of my eye, there was a light that I knew was not quite a firefly, but I had to keep my attention upon my footsteps, especially as twilight was quickly fading into dusk. When I finally reached dry land it was almost completely dark, but I wasn't afraid because there was another, albeit much longer, route that connected with the main highway and then smaller roads that branched off back into town.

I had been walking for over an hour along the highway, asking myself why the unmistakable urge to go to the marsh had been so strong, when Henry Whaling in his long-distance semi almost hurtled past. This was Tuesday, and this was Henry's usual route on Tuesdays. I knew because he had picked me up many times before. I was ready for him this time as well, waving my arms and giving him the thumbs up greeting we had taken to using as our customary hello and goodbye. He slowed down, pulled over and let me in.

The first thing he said after we acknowledged each other was "You know, I just passed the swamp and your fireflies seem very active, much more than I remember. I've seen them before, but to see them so easily from the highway and so many of them—I don't know, but don't you think that's kind of unusual?"

I told him what had happened last night and the feeling in my gut that had sent me out through the marsh and my unscheduled rendezvous with him. What did it matter? I might be reluctant to reveal what I had experienced to others, but Henry was different. He rarely came to town, only passing it by on his way to the various destinations on his preordained itinerary. We soon came to the Greenwich Avenue turnoff, the best way back at this point, and he let me out. I thanked him and just before closing the door told him that maybe I'd see him on the way back. I don't know why I said it because I usually caught him on my way back to town, never on the way out. He never came back the other way. I gave him the thumbs up and watched till he rounded the bend in the highway.

Greenwich was a long meandering road through low hillsides, open meadows, and some small woods, so I still had a fair trek in front of me, plenty of time to consider things further. What Henry had said about the fireflies was rankling. Somehow—I didn't know how—but somehow I knew it was connected to what I had seen and heard and felt. The whisper on the wind, the light out of the corner of my eye, and the itch at the nape of my neck all had a reason and I knew it must be the same reason.

When I finally got back to town, it was almost a quarter to one, and I noticed two individuals under the street lamp near McMurtry's. At first I wasn't sure who they were because I was too far away, and as I approached the intersection their forms dissolved into the dark beyond the corner of the store. But not before I had discovered their identities. It was Edward Blackstone and Mrs. Laughton. Perhaps Mrs. Laughton had forgotten something at McMurtry's, as was not unusual. I rounded the corner but there was no one, not even a light on in the store or above it in Edward's apartment.

The last two days had been long ones for me, so I didn't get up until ten thirty. There wasn't any real urgency to do so as I was on sabbatical from the university, ostensibly to further my research. I went over to the local restaurant/bar and grill for a late breakfast of poached eggs with Worcestershire sauce, sausages, roast pota- toes, brown toast, and coffee. After finishing breakfast and a por- tion of the local paper, I decided that I would take another look at the marsh in the sober light of day, when I wouldn't feel as rushed. This time, for some reason, I felt I would take McGill Avenue to where the tributary passed under the road on its way skirting the fields of the local school. I turned off McGill and walked easily beneath the trees where the land levelled out between the edge of the "Big Hill" and the stream. As kids, in every season, we could almost always be found on that hill having a grand old time. To- boggaining and making snow forts and snowmen in winter, burst- ing milkweed pods so that their parachuting seeds would fill the air in spring, hunting for snakes and exploring or playing cowboys and Indians in summer, and in the fall just passing by it on the way to the Handy Stand to purchase some blackballs or licorice or to discover the new issues of Marvel Comics just come in.

I walked slowly, observing small details—a frog jumping from the edge of the stream to beneath a floating log, a turtle half-sub- merged and almost invisible in his khaki green-brown shell, a red- wing blackbird playing sentinel upon a branch bending under his weight, almost too delicate to hold him. I was looking for some- thing, but I didn't know what. It seemed as if something was in- voluntarily doing the looking for me. I was acutely aware, but felt as if someone else were seeing through my eyes. And I felt a force, a force of purpose or a presence, as if I were being pushed along. I continued along the edge of the stream to a point where, for some reason, apparently clear to whatever it was that was pushing me, it became obvious that I should cross.

It was at this point that I heard the singing, but only for a mo- ment or two, short enough to question whether or not I really had heard it. But distinct enough and unique enough for me not to doubt it in the least. It was very high-pitched though very faint, as though very small birds were singing some distance away. And what they were singing, I was absolutely convinced, were words, barely heard but clear enough. And I was equally convinced these were not words in English.

I crossed to the wet boggy ground on the other side. This was not the best place to cross in my estimation as I could attest to from experience. I had sunk up to my waist once quite near here. But whatever it was that was impelling me was insistent and incessant that I must cross here and I must cross now. The going was definitely much more difficult than last night and much more care needed to be exercised. Thank God it was daytime. It would have been impossible otherwise.

As I laboriously made my way through, I heard something behind me and then felt a breeze pass by and brush my sleeve. I shivered involuntarily and then stopped for everything was absolutely still. Absolutely still. No more breeze, no little creature sounds through the underbrush or in the water, no birds singing, real or otherwise. I even strained my ears to see if I could still hear something from the road in the distance. Even though the road was now invisible, buried behind a curtain of trees and brush and swamp. There was nothing. I took a breath—and a step—and then another, and another. I had gone no more than fifteen paces when again I was short. And there it was. Or rather there it wasn't.

What I didn't see and should have was what we called Birch Island. We usually approached it from the other side where the ground was higher and not as wet. It wasn't exactly an island but there was enough water on three sides of it to make enough of a separation to make it seem like an island. But it wasn't there. In fact nothing was there. All I could see, or not see, was what seemed like heat vapours, the kind that rise off of asphalt highways at the height of summer. But this was May and spring cool and the only thing that should have been there wasn't. I kept trying to see into what looked like sheer glass or the iridescent surface of viscous oil or the mesmeric mirage of lake reflections in the distance.

I stood there transfixed for some moments faced with the impossible dilemma of attempting to look into what could not be seen through. Finally I decided to stop looking and just plunge forward in blind trust. After I pulled myself up out of the water (just where it was supposed to have been had I been able to see it), I looked about among the young birch saplings around me.

Suddenly I noticed that I was able to hear again: the rustling of leaves, birdsong, a mouse scurrying in the grass at my feet. Not seeing anything out of the ordinary, I walked on. The ground rose gently and soon the marsh gave way to meadow. The familiarity of the scene brought me back to the present, at least a more familiar sense of present. I no longer felt the pressure or force that I had felt before, the feeling as if being directed or pushed. I looked back from where I had come and was able to see clearly across the separating waterline that defined one edge of Birch Island. The shimmering wall of iridescent oil was gone as if it had never been. All was as it should be. Or was it?

There was an old abandoned car near the railroad tracks, out past the gravel pit, that we had used as a fort when we were kids. I had come clear of the brush and scrub into the warmth of the unseasonably sunny afternoon that was now beaming upon me, very different from just a little while ago. It would take about forty minutes to get to the fort and, as I really felt the need to be alone right now in order to gather my thoughts, decided that I would go there. It would probably take just long enough for the sun to dry my clothes.

We used to have all kinds of adventures centred around that old abandoned car. We had even made up a code language in order to communicate in secret with each other. I wondered if the codebook were still inside the glove compartment where we always kept it. When I got there the first thing I checked was if it were still there. I couldn't believe it; it was there after all these years. Isn't that something? Partly to still the mind, partly because I was genuinely curious, I opened it up. I tested myself to see if I still remembered some of the things we used to say to each other. Definitely a little rusty but not as bad as might be. I shifted to the back and got comfortable, able to see the train if it came by, able to watch the sun go down if I stayed that long. I wouldn't be. I just wanted some time to come to grips with what was happening. What came to me was just to calm down, return to town, and go about everyday business.

When I got back to town it was two o'clock. But—that was

impossible! It really was impossible. Given everything I had done that day, it should have been closer to five-thirty at least. In order for it to be only two o'clock, I could only have gotten to Birch Island (just before I fell in), turned around, and come back. Everything that happened after could never have happened at all. So what did happen? So much for gathering myself; so much for remaining calm. I found myself looking around, checking for clues as to the location of my wits, checking if anything else were not quite right. I noticed a small crowd in front of McMurtry's.

When I got close enough to distinguish words out of the noise they were making, the first thing I heard was, "He hasn't been seen since eleven-thirty." I gathered they were talking about Ed, who was always punctual and always at McMurtry's during store hours. You could set your watch by it. It was not long after that that I had been at Birch Island. No one had seen Ed in the intervening two-and-a-half hours (an inscrutable six for me).

That night I had a dream. There was a shining light and I either saw or heard—I don't know which—the word Moebius. What was Moebius? There was mist or a full-fledged fog and I saw Ed Blackstone beckoning me towards it and beyond to something just out of reach, just out of sight. When I got to where he had been, I saw him in the distance again, still silently beckoning, and again when I got to the spot where he was, he was gone. I continued through the mist until it started to dissipate and part, revealing a shining luminous object that seemed to glow with its own light. I only saw a portion of it and as soon as my eyes adjusted to the light, words or letters could be made out on the side. I read, M-O-E-B-I-U-S and the dream faded.

When I woke up, at first I didn't remember the dream, and then when I did Edward Blackstone and the word Moebius were prominent. I felt I had to find Ed in order to find out what was going on. McMurtry's was still closed; everyone I asked had no idea where he was, where he had gotten to, what might have happened to him. Mr. McMurtry, who was out of the country, hadn't even been contacted yet. Then I thought, Mrs. Laughton; I hadn't asked her yet. But when I did, she was even less help than if I hadn't found her, for things only became more perplexing.

She was at home at Laughton House and over tea she revealed that she didn't even know who Edward Blackstone was, that she hadn't remembered ever meeting him before, never heard the name before. This was too much even for Mrs. Laughton. She may be a little forgetful, but certainly not an amnesiac. She was actually quite an intelligent woman, in spite of the occasional memory lapse. I delicately mentioned Tuesday night; it didn't jog any remembrance of that evening's events in the least. I allowed the conversation to drift to other topics so as not to unsettle her unnecessarily and then excused myself, saying that I had other errands to attend to and appointments to keep, which was true enough. I still needed to find Ed.

I looked everywhere, asked everyone. Nothing. I was becoming very frustrated, more than a little confounded, and at this point somewhat tired. I returned to my room and lay down for what I thought would be a short nap. When I woke up again it was the middle of the night. I silently cursed myself at the wasted time and got up, washed my face and went out. I retraced my steps of that first night. The fireflies were out in abundance, even more than before. When I got to the marsh and the spots where I had to watch where I placed each footstep, I forced myself to stop and look around. The light that on that previous occasion had merely made its presence felt at the corner of my eye, I now discovered filled the entire sky with an eerie luminescence, almost like the sheen that is displayed as an Aurora Borealis. But this was much closer, more confined to my immediate surroundings, less obvious than northern lights, and yet more pervading.

When I got to the highway, after about a half-hour, there was Henry Whaling's truck barrelling down on me again, which was extremely odd because Henry never came near our town other than on Tuesdays, even had his schedule permitted, and he was heading south again. Why was he headed south? He wouldn't have had time to complete his route and double around. I attempted to wave him down and he drove right past, which was also odd, because Henry was one of the most courteous and helpful people

I had ever met. I watched him round the bend and had a very strange and a very strong sense of déjà vu. I returned to town, but no Edward Blackstone and no Mrs. Laughton. I was at a loss.

The next day I did the same thing the other way, retracing my steps down McGill, along the tributary, past the grove of trees, over the stream to Birch Island. But this time there was something new, perhaps helpful, perhaps even more confusing, definitely out of the ordinary. The birch saplings, for about a fifty-metre radius, had all been flattened to the ground, every one without exception, flattened but unbroken. And even more intriguing, they had all fallen in such a way as to splay in an outward spiralling pattern, as if a small tornado had landed, without destroying anything but affecting everything all the same. I began feeling the same pressure, that same sense of urgency I felt that very first day when I thought I had heard someone calling to me or whispering my name, the same pressure I felt the day when I was impelled to come out here before, as though someone were pushing me. There was the high-pitched birdsong again. And all along the perimeter of Birch Island, right next to the water, there rose a curtain of oil or oil-like substance, iridescent, all around me. I started to feel faint, light-headed and dizzy, and a little nauseated. The last thing I remember was calling out—but I don't remember if it was out loud or only to myself—"Who are you? What are you?" And all I heard, or thought I heard, was the whisper of "Moebius," as if somewhere deep within a conch shell or down a very long corridor someone was calling me.

The first thing I remember I was standing in line at McMurtry's, waiting for Edward Blackstone to finish with Mrs. Laughton. I had gone in to get a Coke and a Hershey's chocolate bar. Ed was the young store manager that McMurtry had hired just last summer. He was new in town, but not so new anymore, and he seemed to be getting on quite well, both as manager of McMurtry's General Goods and as a new citizen to our small town. When Mrs. Laughton left, I heard the jangle of the bells that announced the opening and closing of the front door, the familiar sound that was always somehow so comforting to me.

Your Gladys Crouch is Out There Waiting

Peter Muhvic

Never follow the advice of someone you meet in your dreams. If there is one thing I could bottle up and toss into an ocean it would be that.

I often wonder if somewhere, on some enchanted island, there aren't thousands and thousands of washed up bottles poking out of the sand stuffed with enough juicy thoughts and advice to help piece together the whole meaning-of-life thing. If I could plan my dreams in advance, I'd like to visit that island.

But you can't plan your dreams, at least I can't, which brings me back to my original thought: No matter how smart the people in your dreams may appear, they cannot be trusted. I found this out the hard way, maybe so you don't have to. I'd like to think my grim little tale can result in something positive for someone.

It was during a very deep sleep that I ran into the famous painter Pum Ade. You should know Pum Ade has painted some of the most celebrated works of 21st century art, masterpieces such as *The Curtains are Drapes*, *Transformation in Grey*, and *Your Wish Will Let Somebody Down Somewhere*. You should also know that Pum Ade is a complete fabrication, a dream phantom. Anyway, in my dream he was real enough, and when we collided at the corner of 1st and 1st, the jolt was tangible enough to just about wake me up. Pum Ade, reading the personals section of a newspaper, apologized for not watching where he was going. I too apologized, my excuse being that it was Monday and like every Monday I was wandering the streets with my eyes closed. We had a mild laugh over it all and decided to expand our small chit chat into a full-fledged conversation.

We shuffled off to the nearest coffee shop and grabbed a booth. As it had been raining those plastic hotel room keycards all afternoon, weather was a natural subject to dig into. He had a wonderful anecdote about his stay in a hotel where the maids left a pulsating human heart on his pillow every morning instead of a mint, which I admit was quite amusing. And his delivery was charming enough that, when he leaned forward and arched his brow, I couldn't help but lean forward and lower mine.

"I have something for you," he said. I held out my hand. He blew into it.

"Thanks," I said.

"What I have for you is far more important than some hot air." I understood his gist and blew back into his face. His eyes fluttered like a moth trying to penetrate a light bulb. "Come closer," he said. I nudged forward. "No, even closer." I sat up on my knees, bent forward, and pressed my nose against his forehead. He smelt of porcelain.

"What I have to tell you," he said, in a deep, serious voice that seemed to burrow into my throat and bang away from inside of my neck, "is this and only this: 100% of us have soul mates. 1% of us find them. Seek Gladys Crouch."

"Gladys Crouch," I said softly, not for confirmation, but because I wanted to hear how the name sounded in my voice.

"Yes, Gladys Crouch," Pum Ade repeated, not catching my drift.

I fell back into my seat and clutched my eyes shut. Gladys Crouch. My soul mate was Gladys Crouch. It seemed so obvious at the time. Who else could it possibly be? Any half-wit could see that Gladys Crouch and I were meant to be together forever. Gladys Crouch. What a beautiful, beautiful name.

When I opened my eyes, Pum Ade was gone. The entire coffee shop was gone, in fact, and I was snapped back to my small one bedroom apartment in the city. Just as I sat up and shook off the sleep from my body, the alarm clock rang to life.

I called into work sick for the next two weeks, devoting my every move to finding this woman Pum Ade told me to find.

Gladys Crouch.

I began my search right away and with passion, double and triple checking all my closets, cupboards, and seat cushions. I even quadruple checked my most prized cupboards, as it just felt right that she might turn up there. But alas, my apartment was sadly Gladys Crouch free. I did, however, stumble upon a happily married man who introduced himself as Jacob Mildew. He was tucked away nibbling from my box of Lucky Charms in the cupboard above the fridge, incessantly yammering on about his beautiful wife as milky marshmallows shaped like green clovers dribbled down his mouth and stuck to his shirt. I angrily showed the trespasser the way to the nearest exit.

In my distress I did some squats, assuming that squats would bring about all the Crouchs of the world knocking on my door. But that didn't work either.

I was at a low point. My hunt for Gladys Crouch had started horribly right out of the gate. It had been over two hours and I felt no closer to Gladys Crouch then I did when I began my search.

It dawned on me to check the phone book for somebody who might be able to tell me how to find my soul mate. I scanned under S for soul mate, L for love, and M for me, but nothing was of any apparent help. I took my useless phone book to the bathtub and placed it over the drain. A flip of the tap produced a steady stream of warm water, just as it always did at this time of day (11:23 a.m.), and it was my intention to drown this accursed item filled with worthless pages and meaningless numbers and words. But I couldn't bring myself to go through with it, and promptly freed the soaked but not dead phone book from the tub. I placed it on the sink and tossed a towel over it. "Dry yourself!" I shouted. I may not have had the guts to kill it, but I'd be darned if I was going to play nurse for it.

I ran into the kitchen and gobbled down some pie I made the night before, choking on its apple innards because I was so out of breath from running from the bathroom to the fridge. It was good pie. It tasted like apples, only covered in sugar and cooked and warm and soft, which, when you think about it, doesn't taste at all like apples.

Oh, if only I could go on and on thinking about pie all day. But Gladys Crouch, the elusive Gladys Crouch, was sitting on my brain, shouting into my ears from the inside that I needed to find her, the sooner the better of course.

"You need to find me," she shouted, "the sooner the better of course!" Her voice sounded like Billie Holiday's dipped in gold and chocolate.

I made a tin can phone out of a length of string and two cans that contained pineapple slices. I held one can up to my mouth and the other up to my ear. "I want to," I said to myself. "Just tell me how! I beg you!" But the voice in my head didn't tell me what to do, so I ate pineapple slices instead.

My stomach soon felt the way my spirits did, and I spent the rest of the afternoon hovering over the bathtub fully expecting to fill it with chewed up apple pie, pineapple slices, and anything else appley that my tummy had in it. But I couldn't even do that right, and in time I got bored with the fruitless anticipation and stepped into the tub to take a nap. I'm not sure if I was sleeping or awake when I noticed the towel by the sink, and really, it doesn't much matter. The important thing is lives are changing every second of every day. Except if you're a human statue: then I imagine things are pretty much always the same.

Anyway, I noticed the towel and that made me think about the phone book underneath it. Something told me to give it another look-see. I got up and took the towel in my hands, instinctively drying off even if I was fully clothed and not at all wet. The phone book seemed to glow, like kinda just flicker and stuff, and then I saw that the source was the dying light bulb over my head and not some superpower the phone book exuded. I flipped open the phone book and thumbed my way to the C's. Placing a call to Willis Crouc, my light bulb guy, was now the priority.

As my index finger worked up the page, passing all the Crumps, Cruickshanks, and Crowders the city had, I was stunned, positively stunned, to see the name Crouch sitting right there at my fingertip. There were two entries under that name: Crouch G and Crouch G.

I grabbed the emergency phone I kept under the bathroom sink for such occasions as this (I knew it would come in handy one of these days) and immediately dialed. In my nervousness I must have dialed up a combination of both Crouch G numbers, so shaky was my finger on the page, for on the other line was not Crouch G but The Swedish Food and Hobby Shop.

"Swedish Food and Hobby Shop, Tes speaking, how can I help you?" the velvety voice on the other line purred, whatever that means.

"Hi," I nervously responded. "I'd like to speak to Gladys Crouch."

"Gladys Crouch? I'm sorry, there's no one by that name here."

"You're Tes Crouch, correct?"

"Incorrect. You got the Tes part right."

"Awesome!"

"Sir, my last name isn't Crouch. It's Oulma."

"Oh, I see."

"So do you want some Swedish food?"

"Uh...okay. Do you have a special or something?"

"We specialize in specials. Wanna try the knäckebröd with apple sauce?"

"Well, when you put it that way..."

"Great. How about a hobby? Would you like a Swedish hobby?"

"Um, sure, okay, yeah."

"I can teach you to play brännboll?"

"That sounds fine."

"I'll be right over with your meal and some paddles."

"And don't forget Gladys Crouch."

"No Gladys Crouch here."

"Worth a shot, right?"

Tes hung up before she could answer. I put the phone down and went to the door because that's where I kept my door handle. Three hours later Tes showed up.

"You forgot to tell me your address," Tes said in a matter-of-fact way.

"Oh, I live at—"

"I know where you live. Here, right?"

"Right!"

"You didn't have to answer that."

"I see. So then how did you find me?" I asked, both of us still standing at the door.

"I...I don't know. I just started walking, and every step started to feel more and more right, like something was pulling me, but in a way I wasn't really being pulled because I was so eager to get to where I was going and moving so fast that I eventually overtook the thing that was doing the pulling and I started to pull it. And I ended up here. I can't explain how, but I knew I would. I think maybe we were meant to meet and maybe we just needed a little help." She smiled like she meant it, which is exceedingly rare these days and a truly beautiful thing. I smiled back. I meant it too.

We ate the Swedish special and I tried my hand at a little brännboll. We also talked a fair deal, which is worth noting because usually when company comes over not a single word is exchanged. She told me how she once had a dream about going to a movie theater to watch a sequel to *Big Trouble in Little China* called *Bigger Trouble in Little China*. I told her about the dream I had where I went to a movie theater to watch a sequel to her sequel called *Same Sized Trouble in a Suddenly Big China*. We were so amazed we couldn't help it and high-fived.

I wanted to put some music on, but my record player was broken. That didn't stop us from dancing, though, and we took turns singing songs by one-hit wonders into each other's ear. It was a magical night, and not just because I did some card tricks for her.

I believe it's possible to fall madly in love because Tes and I are proof of it. Ah, but every cloud that has a silver lining is still a big old ice crystal filled thunderstorm brewing cloud, and my cloud here is that somewhere out there Gladys Crouch, my soulmate, is quadruple checking her cabinets for me not knowing that I have officially called off the search.

The Doppelganger

Jerry Levy

With four words—*I won't miss you*—Mitchell Black's wife walked out of his life. She could hardly be blamed. He wasn't interested in much, never wanted to go anywhere. He was, if truth be known, a bore. The verbal assault sent Black on a fast downward spiral, one greased with tranquilizers and anti-depressants.

Some four months later and in a sober moment, Black reasoned that since it was his wife who had thrown him into this decrepit state, she could reverse his misfortunes with just a few kind words. Perhaps those *four words* were not truthful, that they had been spoken in the heat of the moment—that was his hope.

He decided to show up at her door unannounced. She could hardly turn him away then. So feeling remarkably well but at the same time extraordinarily nervous, he hopped on a bus and began the journey.

As he got closer to her house, he began to experience pangs of doubt and his heart raced. He sucked at the air in big, uneven gulps and tried to collect himself. The street was quite dark; the lamplights on one side had been turned off and Black's long, dark shadow slanted obliquely across the road, giving him the appearance of a mythical giant.

His legs felt soft and wobbly and he had to make a conscious effort to move one foot in front of the other. The dimly lit house suddenly appeared before him and he stood rigidly before it. Black paced back and forth for a time and then stealthily crept into the shrubbery. Moving forward on his hands and knees, he sidled up to the front window and peeked in. Intertwined arms and legs, a hand riding up his wife's skirt. Hungry, smacking lips. A fluid connection between hips. "Just touch me!" he heard his wife scream. "Kiss me again!" He continued to watch for a few minutes longer and then, when he felt his heart would explode from his chest cavity, he pulled himself away and staggered back to the sidewalk, where he proceeded to spew bile in long arcs.

Tears clouded his eyes and his nose dripped. The taste of acid soured his insides. Perhaps this was all understandable. After all, he had just witnessed his wife making love to a man. Not just any man. No, firmly and passionately embraced within his wife's arms was none other than a man who looked exactly like himself!

Returning home, he read the labels on his pill bottles through misty eyes, gulped twice as many as he normally did, drank a glass of red wine and sprawled lifeless into bed with his clothes on.

The following day, Black muddled through the day at Barnes & Sellers Ad Agency where he worked as an accounts payable clerk, barely able to concentrate. Riding the elevator down, he gasped when the very man he saw making love to his wife walked in. The second Mr. Black stood impassionate next to the original. As the elevator doors slid open at the ground floor, the original, his jaw slack with awe, walked out first, his copy close behind. And as the original kept turning to ogle the second Mr. Black, the latter had no option but to say "You're staring at me. Do I know you?" The original however, walked on without answering.

That night, the original Mr. Black spent frenzied hours on the Internet, researching the idea of a double. He had never seen anyone resemble him as closely as did the second Mr. Black; it was, for him, eerily uncanny, unearthly. He stumbled across the German for a double, otherwise known as a 'doppelganger'. He read with dismay that doppelgangers often appear in a person's life as a foreshadowing of death and that others can't see the imposter.

The next day the original Mr. Black made some inquiries and found out that his nemesis was Roland Ewen, the new head of the advertising department. He suspected that the best way to deal with Ewen was to get close to him, watch his every move and then spring a surprise on him when he least expected it. What exactly that surprise was, he had no clue. How to get close was equally problematic since the two worked in different departments—their paths would never cross. All throughout the day Black ruminated over his options and got nary a scintilla of work done.

After sleeping fitfully, Black once again called in sick to work and instead went straight to the library. The idea that Black hatched was to change departments. To do so, he would have to show the people in the know that he was worthy of working in the creative department that Ewen headed-up. He would steal creative ideas and pass them off as his own—that was the plan.

In the library, he found a series of advertising magazines entitled *Communication Arts Advertising Annual*, which featured the best and most innovative ads of the year. Black selected an older magazine, going back to 1996, and thumbed his way through the multitude of slick ads. He reasoned that 1996 was old enough—no one would remember the ad, provided, that is, that he changed a word here and there.

And then he saw them: two ads for BMW featuring fuzzy pictures of motorcyclists, their leather-clad bodies and bikes a blur of motion. The first ad read:

And yet,
The rider will remember this moment with perfect clarity.
The second ad said:
Not available with cupholders, baby seats, or cellular phones.
Ever.

He would change them around a bit and then claim authentic ownership: no one would know that he hadn't produced them. Mitchell Black, budding copywriter, budding creative genius. First he changed them to bicycle ads.

The first ad now read:

The ride is a blur.
But the rider will recall this moment with perfect clarity.

The second ad was changed to this:

Not equipped with baby seats, coffeeholders, or cellular phones.
Never.

It was the best he could do under the circumstances. His mind was as empty as deepest interstellar space. Looking through cycling magazines, he found a picture of a fast cyclist on a track, which he photocopied. Then he proceeded with the copy above the picture. When he was finished, he examined his handiwork with much pride, amazed and excited at his own ingenuity.

The next day, Black walked into his boss' office and asked for a transfer into the copywriting department. He explained that he needed a change, felt an urge to grow, and wanted to explore his more creative side. He presented his work for consideration. His voice shook as he spoke, primarily because he didn't have a creative bone in his body, was adverse to change of any sort, and had done all the growing that he believed he could.

Over the next few weeks, Black's health continued to worsen. He was chronically fatigued, anxious, suffered from insomnia, ate only sardines from a can, felt achy in his bones, and would simply collapse upon coming home from work. Moreover, his depression seemed to become more oppressive, darker, and his mind busier—a virtual highway of disjointed thoughts.

Three weeks after the request had been put in, Black got his answer. His request would be granted. He would become a junior copywriter.

※　※　※

Thirty-five year old Roland Ewen had been at Barnes & Sellers two months. Prior to that, he was a coveted freelance copywriter, with some twelve years in the business. He had worked on major accounts such as Coca-Cola, Tide, Nabisco, Carlsberg, Air Canada, Starbucks, Microsoft, and Proctor & Gamble.

On the Sunday night prior to starting his new job, Mitchell was in a state of near-hysteria. Disparate random thoughts bombarded his beleaguered mind. He did not for a moment believe that he could actually work in a creative atmosphere and felt that while he had somehow miraculously duped those who agreed to the job switch, he would eventually be found out. In the morning he listened to the radio and heard the marine forecast:

Red sky at night,
Sailor's Delight
Red sky at Dawn,
Sailor be Warned.

As Black rode the elevator to the lobby, he chanted those words over and over again, like a mantra. And as the weather forecast had predicted, the red sky at dawn turned nasty; it parted, cracked open, and a steady fine rain fell down on top of Black's heavy head, whipped by swift winds.

Monday morning at Barnes & Sellers was the weekly meeting for the creative team; the very one Black was joining. It was at these meetings that ideas were exchanged, target markets determined, and decisions made as to who would work certain accounts. It was a time to sparkle, where tentative ideas evolved into great slogans and campaigns, where even junior copywriters sometimes outshone their more experienced counterparts.

Roland Ewen looked at his watch. "Has anyone seen the new guy, the one from accounting?"

No one had.

"Well, let's get started. We can't wait forever," he said.

When Black eventually walked into Ewen's office, twelve minutes late, he was met by eight set of eyes, four men's, three women's and of course Ewen's. There was an art director, account executive, two copywriters, and various assistants. They were all fairly young (twenties and thirties) and highly creative. Black, in his late forties, was the oldest in the group.

As he made his way sheepishly into the room, he noticed that they were all casually dressed—torn jeans, running shoes, and baseball caps turned backwards. Black, dressed in his best gray suit from his accounting days, felt awkward, overdressed, outdated, or something. The sweet sweep of his hair that he used to hide a part of his balding head suddenly felt limp and drooped lazily into his eyes. He was introduced around and told to watch.

"Okay, let's initiate for Mitchell's sake," said Ewen. "Let's do the ideas game."

A woman pulled out an obviously ripped pair of pantyhose from her schoolbag and held them up against a wall clock. "A rip in time saves nine," she crackled as she moved the hands of the clock to nine o'clock.

"That is one ripping good yarn," someone else sang out.

The phrases came from all parts of the room, too quickly for Black. He couldn't fathom what they were getting at. He listened intently but was perplexed. Ewen told Black that they often worked that way, just to create slogans. He grabbed a copy of the Sunday New York Times and handed it to Black.

"Here, why don't you look through this and tell us which ad appeals to you."

Black began looking while the rest of the group discussed ongoing ad campaigns. Page after page of high-tech computers, sweet smelling perfumes, chic urban clothes, flowery herbal shampoos, scrumptious Belgian chocolates, designer eyeglasses, smooth liquors, beers, fine art supplies, creamy pastries, fabulous fabrics, big comfy sofas, pure silk Persian rugs, white goose down duvets. A whole glittery world in the New York Times and yet for Black, it was all grey. Nothing appealed to him.

He felt hot and loosened his tie. He looked around and saw that no one was paying him any heed. They were all engrossed in *their* thing, whatever that was. Lunatics, absolute bloody lunatics. He watched Roland Ewen with particular interest. Animated but in control. Poised. It was clear that he was the leader of the group. You could just tell. How could Ewen make love to *his* wife? Did Ewen think he could have whatever he wanted? Did Ewen think his wife was like one of those Belgian chocolates? The more he watched him, the more he hated Roland Ewen, the second Mr. Black and a true imposter. That handsome face of Ewen...his very own face.

The group's conversation fizzled down, decisions were made. Black found one ad for oversized golf umbrellas that he didn't mind. It showed a pack of golfers holding them up in showery weather while they continued their round. The caption read: *Neither rain, nor sleet.* An ordinary scene, ordinary men (although he was no golfer) ...just like him.

"It's understated," offered Black.

Ewen held the ad up for the others.

"Now how would you make it better?"

Ewen's question took him by surprise. Critical eyes were upon him. He blurted out the first thing that came to mind: "*Instead of neither rain nor sleet, I'd say* 'Red sky at night, Sailor's delight. Red sky at dawn, Sailor be warned.'"

Someone tried to suppress a laugh, but it came out all the same. Then someone else snickered. In no time at all, the walls of the room were vibrating, rocking with laughter.

Ewen chuckled. "Everybody gets razzed around here."

"Don't take it to heart," someone else chimed in.

Black felt like an outsider, an old man in a young man's world, the world of ideas, of which he had none. He stared hard at Ewen and every fibre in his body, every single atom, felt taut and on edge. His eyes turned wild, his eyebrows folded together into a scowl and he became instantly crazy. He lunged at Ewen with arms flailing away madly. Ewen, much taller at six feet two inches than his combatant and in fabulous physical condition, easily eluded Black and flung him to the ground at which time the latter struck out with his legs. One kick and then a second...others followed in a rapid staccato fashion. With each kick deflected, another found its mark on Ewen's shins. Black, an uncontrollable bucking bronco, would not stop and was quickly set upon by every single person in the room.

Everything stopped. Black sat sprawled on the floor, his nose bleeding and his chest heaving. All eight people in the room stepped back and let him rise painfully to his feet. "I'm sorry," said Black. He straightened his shirt and pants and pulled his sweep of hair up onto his head. "But not so much," he continued. "Know why? Cause the rain in Spain falls mainly on the plain. Or how about this: Sippity sup, Sippity sup, bread and milk from a china cup."

"Just relax Mr. Black," said Ewen. "You've caused enough damage for one day."

"Me, caused damage? Me? You're the one who started this all!"

"How do you mean?" asked Ewen, perplexed.

"You were the one who was making love to my wife, just when I wanted to reconcile!"

Ewen sighed. "I'm sorry, Mr. Black, but you've got me confused with someone else. I'm married with kids. My wife is in fact sitting right there." He pointed to a pretty blond woman.

Like a sailor's ship slamming into a squall, Ewen's words, much like his wife's four months earlier, sent Black spinning into netherland. Red sky at dawn indeed. He shakily grabbed a handful of pills from his pocket and threw them down his throat.

"That's a lot of pills Mr. Black," someone said, concerned.

"Never enough," he mumbled. He reached into his other pocket and pulled out another handful, which he proceeded to swallow. The pills went down hard, jagged rocks tumbling through a mineshaft.

"Water, water," he gasped and reached for a pitcher on the table, from which he drank in great big gulps.

And just at that moment, when Black was thinking of another nursery rhyme that he might spout out to save himself, he noticed something highly unusual. He gazed from one stern face to the next and saw that all the men looked remarkably like him, each and every one. A flash of some revelation entered into his frazzled mind and a deep sadness began to creep through him: Mitchell Black wondered how in the world he had ever become the kind of man that people actually look at.

The Stones

Lindsay R. Allison

Lindsay Allison

A long time ago, my Granddad told me that the tide washed away the troubled souls of those who died. On the very quietest of summer evenings, when the sky is laced with pink cotton clouds and the flaming red sun begins to dip beyond the horizon, the souls who carry immense pain and grief begin to gather. Whether from some brilliant unknown supernatural force or by coincidence, souls who carry similar burdens end up flocking together as one giant mass of surreal energy to head toward the afterlife.

The reasons for the tragic events during their lives quickly become clear, and most souls openly accept the causes for their anguish. As soon as their suffering is embraced and understood, the spirits never pause or hesitate when the wind eventually floats over the sea to brush upon them gently.

When the sun sets, the spirits who carry acceptance feel elated. Then the Wind God gently closes its hand around them, coaxes them, and guides them soothingly forward to the afterlife. A feeling of great exhilaration and bliss unlike anything imaginable to the living can be heard during this event through the sighs and movements of the tide, as it breathes heavily in and out with the sweet sounds of eternal life.

As the souls bask in elevated happiness, and while the Wind pulls them peacefully along, they see to the left of them along the horizon the most recent life they had lived. To the right of the horizon they see their destiny, as clear as an intricately painted picture on canvas. In the middle of the sky, where the sun was once suspended near the water, holds a beaming white light as the portal to the afterlife. Below them is a footpath of giant flat stones that leads out into the middle toward the light. The souls see the Stones. The living only sees the waves.

Sometimes the sun sets long into the night and there are still spirits who do not accept the hardship they encountered during their lifetime. These souls who willingly or mistakenly miss their opportunity to depart are stranded within the realms of the Earth until there is another peaceful summer evening along the seashores. The spirits who missed far too many chances to depart are usually the most corrupted and evil ghost-like entities one may encounter on Earth; they have too long been shunned from the necessities hidden in the afterlife. Granddad said to always keep a far distance from these creatures if they were ever confronted, for they pleasured in corrupting and causing harm to others.

The living are not supposed to stand anywhere near the water once the sun begins to set, for if they were, they would drown from the impeccable weight of the spirits' energy. When my parents were very young and very much in love, they wandered too far onto the shore and were suffocated by the heaviness of the souls. The sea swallowed them, leaving me to my Granddad and to my quiet, intolerable misfortune.

I was six years old when my Granddad first told me the story of the Stones. I don't know if he made it up when I asked him what lie beyond the sea, or if it was fiction to supply my desperate need to discover my parents' death. Whatever the reason was, I accepted the story, drinking everything in desperately. I was a needy child with not much to live for, but in my mind I was so free and alive, so full of imagination, and nothing would stop me from trying to research or hunt down information I wanted to know.

But my free-spirited nature all changed on the day of my

eighth birthday, when I tried to find the Stones for myself. I was so enchanted by the words of Granddad's tale that it became an obsession and a daily thought. The combination of naturally being rambunctious and the excitement that it was my birthday brought up courage in me that I would probably never possess today. On the morning of June the twenty-first, 1989, I was determined to seek out the Stones, but felt only foamy water around my legs just below the knees.

Maybe I had ventured too deeply that day, for the waves smacked violently against my calves as if they were angry, and the sky held clouds that were so dark and menacing I could not see any blue. Disappointed and offended, I frowned like a naughty boy into the heavens. As if the God of the Wind himself saw me, a huge gust of air suddenly blew right at me. When it hit my face, the air itself was so cold and wet that it stung my cheeks and I had to turn my head the other way. I remember feeling like a very small boy being disciplined, and all I could see then were my flying chunks of thick black hair flap madly in the wind. On that day I became forever frightened of the water and anything that may be possessed by it.

I remember running back toward land shortly afterward, feeling cautious, wondering if the waves had flushed me backwards as a warning of some kind. When I turned around to flash a final cunning look at the waters, the waves curled in and roared at me. It was as if it was sending me a signal, trying to remind me that I could not pass nor survive in its depths. I had the distinct feeling it knew what I was thinking. I never looked for the Stones again.

When I found my love Sedna, my life finally began to make sense. We loved each other so much; the village people knew, Granddad knew, everyone knew, and when she agreed to marry me it was the happiest day of my life.

On the day of our wedding, we were to get married on a beautiful boat. It was her choice, as she would marry the ocean herself if I didn't come into her life. I knew it was a bad idea but would do anything to make my love happy on our wedding day.

Before the sermon there was a terrible storm. The ship rocked and swayed heavily. I never saw her plunge to her death, but from what I heard she slipped on the deck and fell overboard. She died almost instantly; being in a heavy wedding dress, and having the stormy waves crash over her head. They tried to save her, but she had gone under and we had to bring the boat back to shore. It was a cruel irony, really, to have my future wife taken from me as well as everything else. I think the Gods must hate me.

Since then I have been thrown into a deep depression. To this day, the locals and village people know never to mention that catastrophic event when I'm around. I have never been the same since. Seeing her in spirit form is almost as upsetting as seeing her die.

It is half past eleven now and I finally notice how tired I am. My crooked old bed creaks underneath the weight of me as I sit on it, clutching the same large browned envelope I have been holding since ten o'clock this morning. It is not only filled with about six hundred photographs from my early childhood, but also filled with long forgotten feelings of emotion that I only remembered again once I opened the package. I see Granddad's smiling face beaming back at me from one of the photos. This one was taken back in 1983, when his skin was especially dark, when his hair was not yet fully grey, and when he was wearing that brown leather vest I liked. I can see the old layout of the back of my cabin, with the old canoes lying on the sand and the deep-green forested area to the right. I squint to observe the background. It looks like the ocean and sky are young, vibrant, innocent and calm like my Granddad standing still in the foreground. But then my mind retreats back to the present, and I am only holding a picture that is yellowing and smells stale.

Granddad was always telling me to go chase my dreams, to always try hard in life and never give up. He was an important figurehead in my life, being the one who raised me and having no family but him. I had sort of a fantasy dream when I was young—I thought I wanted to go university, or maybe college, and pave a path that neither my parents nor he ever could. Six days ago I received a letter that I had been accepted at a university down in

British Columbia. I wasn't even sure if I wanted to go, but Grand-dad said I should try it out. After many petty brawls, I finally agreed to go. By a freak coincidence, or one could say destiny, Granddad died the day after I flew down to tour the campus.

Maybe it was God's way of letting him go peacefully without my worry. The local police said he passed away in his sleep three short days ago, a wise old man with love in his heart.

I decided I was not going to pursue school; knowing myself, that would get me nowhere but in debt, and in the end I'd only end up back in the place I love the most: Home. I stayed up for most of the two nights that passed, not knowing where to go or what to do, feeling angry and distraught. Since I have no other family, the locals and police said they'd help me clear out his things in the old cabin, but I shunned them to do it myself. In his will he left everything for me, anyway.

Sadly, I thought the Stones would actually appear to me when I arrived back home. I was conceited and angry enough to think I had the privilege to see them while I was still alive. I shouted at all the Gods and screamed and cursed at them, but they weren't nice enough to let me chase after my Granddad along the Stones so I could at least say goodbye. But there were no Stones. The water merely seemed to stare back at me, tide pulling and pushing calmly as the sun set below the horizon.

Beer bottles are lying carelessly on the moth-eaten carpet floor around me, accompanied with used wine glasses and an almost-empty bottle of rye. How I wish I could understand the sea, even though I am so afraid of it. The photograph I am clutching makes my hand shake.

The Goddess of the Sea is a beautiful mermaid who can take any form in which she likes in order to control the beasts and spirits in the water. Granddad said she was always longing for a husband, so tends to entice vulnerable men to come into the sea with her so they can spend eternity together in love, controlling spirits. Granddad told me that he had met her once, and that she had tried to take him swimming. I think I only believed him because I was young and liked to hear stories that would give me hope for something more.

My grandfather also told me that, when he should die, he would wait for me until the most peaceful and beautiful of summer evenings carries us along to the afterlife together. I beamed at him at those words but then thought otherwise.

But Granddad, I told him fearfully. If you wait for me, you will miss many turns when the wind comes to pull you along. You may become a corrupted spirit if you choose to wait for me. You're so much older than I am!

He said nothing but only chuckled at me and ruffled up my coarse black hair.

I continue sitting on the bed, waiting for my love to arrive.

I hear stirring over to my left, and sigh with some relief when Sedna shimmers into view on my right hand side. However, mostly I feel grief and a pang of pain in my heart when she arrives. I am used to her doing this, as she checks in on me frequently since the day she died. My eyes are drooping and are so very dry, but the night air welcomes me through the window and soothes me, feeling warm and smelling grassy. The crickets can be heard, as the shutters are open all the way.

I suddenly hear My Spirit Guide cautioning me, but this is not unusual as she usually does this when Sedna comes around. She may have reason to, but as I am not in the right state of mind at the moment I don't bother to listen, nor can I understand the meaning behind her words.

I smell the sweet air and look at Sedna, who has her long back slightly turned toward me. The outline of her body glows brighter than the moonlight. Her cream-coloured dress is woven neatly over her waist and falls gracefully down to the floor, pinned up at certain places where the roses are tucked neatly inward. I can see the pieces of material along her back that are as thin as baby flower stems, crossed over many times to form a sort of corset. Around her arms are cream-coloured gloves. Some of her auburn hair has fallen out of her pins and hangs loosely in waves at her sides so that they touch past her shoulders.

Careful, someone says. Some spirits are not to be trusted.

Sedna's eyes fall upon the shadow of my dark figure. I don't think she can see me clearly, for she never looks into my eyes. But I can see hers. They are dark, green and remind me of the sea. "Kinapak." She says my name, gliding over to me. Sometimes I am scared of her newly freakish movements and the abnormal greenish haze in her eyes that only recently developed, but tonight everything about her seems different and somewhat enticing.

"I have come to bring you somewhere," she turns around and whispers into my ear, half-closing her dark eyes. I can hear the spirits of the Earth whispering, the realms quivering and the Earth rumbling, but it falls into my ears like sweet music. I follow her out the door and into the moonlight. Something is different about tonight. A voice tells me something is wrong, but I refuse to believe it.

I am sleepy and fearful. My Spirit Guide, though I cannot see her, echoes warnings in my ear. It is all dark and dangerous here, and yet I follow Sedna. She is walking through the forest, laughing her sweet laugh. I desire to catch her, and I run excitedly behind her through the trees.

The spirits of the Earth cackle madly at me and swoop all around so that I see black whips of movement everywhere. They are trying to distract me but my desire to be with Sedna overcomes their cries. I can still see the edge of her dress, trailing trough the underbrush through the confusing swarms of Earth spirits.

"Tonight's the night!" I hear her ahead say hysterically in a high-pitched, clear voice so unlike her own. Most of the spirits have cleared off now. Something is scaring them.

I soon find out why the spirits have retreated. There is a quick, blinding flash of light and Sedna, who I now see clearly ahead of me at the water's edge, has vanished, only to be replaced by the most beautiful mermaid I have ever seen. She has a huge glistening fin and wet wildflowers tangled in her carefree hair.

I fall to my knees. This is not Sedna but an illusion—a ploy to lure me through even the most dark and dangerous of nights.

My knees sink into the sand as I begin to cry like a frightened boy. I am afraid. The Goddess of the Sea slips into the water and begins to sing such sweet, lulling, beautiful music only to me. Her sensual sea green eyes beckon me to her.

Her voice is the most enchanting sound I have ever heard. I am delighted. I find I want to go near, to slip into the water myself and be embraced by her.

Suddenly, like a crack of a whip, an image of Granddad's laugh beams right in front of my eyes, breaking the trance.

Then all is silent. I find that I am completely confused and dumbfounded as to how I ended up so close to the water at such an important time. I feel a need to run, to get out as fast as I can, but at the same time I do not want to move. I stand up and look out into the ocean. My mermaid is gone.

Everything seems like it has stopped. Something pulls me forward, but I pull back.

"What's going on here?" I shout into the air, and the Wind carries it along into the distance where it is drowned in the now roaring sea. The clouds above have quickly blackened and become thick and puffy, swirling threateningly around in vicious circles beyond the horizon.

Thunder crackles and I see the flash of illumination lightning has created. I am mad and possessed. For some reason I feel the urge to run towards the water, to see if I can get a short glimpse of the Stones and maybe Granddad. The Wind has become so ferocious that more tears stream against my cheeks as I run against it, ignoring more serious, frightened protests from my Spirit Guide. My feet sink through the sand so quickly I fear it's trying to swallow me up, but I refuse to let it devour me.

I hear the howling and whistling of the Wind God all around me. He is steadily blowing me backwards and soon I can hear nothing but his giant breath against me. But I am fearless and determined for the first time since the summer solstice on my eighth birthday. I think nothing will hurt me, however I quickly change my mind when I realize I have come within feet of the edges of the water. I am suddenly extremely scared. Before I can react the Wind stops blowing against me and changes directions so fast I swear it's like giant hands pulling me forward. Once it stops I fall face-first, exhaling a great amount of air.

I stumble in the damp sand. Something is odd because the Wind God has stopped breathing, and now when I look up the sea has stopped churning. Even the clouds have stopped swirling and are replaced with the setting rays of the sun. Everything seems completely still. The water is now making calm slopping noises right in front of my spread-eagled fingers.

Silence. More tears fall down my cheek. I moan in grief and sadness, wondering why all that is good has to be taken away. I am thinking thoughts of despair when a sudden movement of the light flickers against the corner of my eye.

Spirits. Tons of them. They are flocking by the hundreds and are coming my way.

I scramble to get out of the way but I do not know where I am. I am frantically pushing my way through the crowds, but none seem to neither hear me nor care. My head is spinning; the energy around me is so strong, so surreal. I can literally feel the emotions within the millions of spirits around me bleed through my very skin, and I don't know whether to laugh, cry, be angered, weep with joy, or to be confused or heartbroken. The sounds of eternity are humming loudly in my ears. I can hear cries, laughter, and heartbreak. I don't even feel like a person, but a being.

After what seems like hours, I find that my body is lying on the cool sand. My vision is very blurred but I am lying there peacefully, for some reason not particularly concerned about anything at all. Everything is moving slower than usual; I find this logical.

Warm light rests upon my face, and I find that I am starting to close my eyes. I smile to myself and wonder what's so amusing, but I cannot find the answer. I am just so eternally happy. Looks like most of the spirits are gone.

My breathing becomes slow and very peaceful. For a second I see for the first time the charming face of my Spirit Guide floating upwards to take my hand. She looks at me earnestly, and this time I hear her voice clearly:

"Didn't screw up again this time. What do you think, Kakray-ok?" She turns and smiles to someone.

Kakrayok? The name is familiar and I smile broadly. I can hear the waves again but they are not frightening. Rather calming.

"I think he's splendid. Tell me, Kinapak. Was that such a long wait after all?"

I tilt my head up to see Granddad. He is ever so young looking and beaming at me. I find that I have stood up so fast it felt like I soared a million miles.

"Long wait?" I repeat breathlessly, looking at him in admiration. "What do you mean?" I gaze dreamily at my Spirit Guide.

"Yeah," he said, taking my hand and guiding me along soothingly, like the wind would if it had fingers. "You know. Now you'll finally get to see them."

I see Granddad hovering above the tide ahead of me, but this time I am following and he is laughing and smiling. I look over to the right and see the final pink and orange rays of the setting sun, intricately woven with my destiny. To the left I see my childhood.

Then I see the Stones.

The Deer Path

Sarah Patterson

T he heavy smell of oak trees was the first to reach his senses, followed shortly by the sharp autumn air that made his anatomy cringe in discomfort. After a few moments of this sensual entertainment, wisps of colour began to fill his vision, almost as if God was trying to pour his mystical acrylics into his blackened soul. Brown first, then orange; then drips of green. God must have preferred impressionism.

As time passed, the young man began to make out his surroundings from the smudges of colour. A forest. On what seemed to be a deer path. He wiggled his toes on the soft, mossy ground and marvelled at his ability to move his icy joints. He was slowly coming back to earth now. Slowly.

However, as he stood there dumbfounded, he still remained powerless to detect any sort of noise or movement. There was a sort of pressure that he felt on all sides of his body, not a physical pressure, but more the kind that he couldn't explain—or even understand.

This feeling seemed to affect everything. There was not a single sound, not a single shift in the environment; just a heavy pulsing of mysterious sensations.

Then, as if he was a withering child under the surface of the water, he was let free. The weighted veil was removed from the face of the forest, and even though it was liberated, it lacked the needed kiss from the autumn sun. He was breathing now, along with the wind that sighed through the crooked oaks.

Normalcy.

The young man raised his right hand and grasped the small tree beside him. It held him up as he suffered a small sensation rush, sort of like the feeling one would get from standing up too quickly. He didn't remember standing up however, just a funny feeling. He concentrated on the deer path.

After a few moments, his groggy brain registered a funny taste in his mouth, and he quickly raised his left hand to his lips. He discovered blood, his own, oozing from both his nostrils. Shocked, he reached down to his sweater—the makeshift tissue—but grasped only at his bare chest.

He looked down to discover his naked condition. There was not a shred of clothing on his pasty body, not even briefs to secure his dignity. No wonder he was shivering like a baby.

Staring flabbergasted at his adolescent skin, he pried his brain for an explanation. *Where am I? What am I doing here?* He stood motionless for what seemed like hours, gaping at his bellybutton. He suffered another head rush, and red paint dripped on his white belly. God had made a mistake.

He finally looked up, down the twisted deer path. He had an insane desire to follow it; all the way to the end.

He was going to do just that—after a short rest.

Numbed joints screamed in discomfort as he kneeled down to the forest floor, all the while keeping his hand firmly on the tree. He was afraid of falling and piercing his sensitive skin with a rock or jagged branch. He was already bleeding enough.

The moss was soft under his buttocks, yet the chilling touch only escalated his shivering, and he concluded it would be wise if he did not stay for long. He decided that his next destination would be down the deer path, as if he knew what his previous destination had been. He had no reconciliation of his whereabouts, other than his vague understanding that he was in Canada—somewhere in Canada. The chilled air, the lack of sunshine, and the interesting colours littered amongst the tree leaves informed him that autumn was here, and its evening frost would not be forgiving to his condition.

Upon observing his surroundings, the young man's heart swelled with loneliness, which happened to be his first predominant emotion since his awakening. *Alone in a forest, with no idea of what's going on. Good combination.*

Time passed, and eventually he got up and started down the deer path. He walked slowly at first to avoid hurting his feet. He decided that his best bet would be to follow the path to the end, where hopefully lay a road of some sort, or a lake where people resided. He thought of several excuses for his odd behaviour, ones that he would eventually tell to the people who found him. He realized his excuses would not go far, especially if he did not even know his own name.

He wondered if he was on drugs. He did not know much about himself, but he did know that the sole word "drug" sounded repulsive and disgusting to him. If it was drugs that did this to him, then he had not taken them willingly.

Drugs or no drugs, he was still lost in a forest.

He spent an hour or two venturing down the path. He often turned his head to the sky, looking for a possible break, so he would know approximately how long he had until dark. However, from what he could see through the branches, there was no chance that he would see daylight; the dark clouds hung low.

Despair washed over him. He stopped and buried his face in his hands, weeping. *Jesus! What am I going to do?* He sat on the ground again, not caring about its icy touch. *I don't even know who I am! What's happening to me?* His mind was so groggy, so filled with empty holes. He could not remember a single thing about himself.

More time passed, and after awhile, he had no tears left to cry. His stomach growled and he kept moving along the path, trying to think about what he was going to eat.

Eventually, he found a muddy creek running alongside the

deer path. While he washed the dried blood from his face, something peculiar happened.

First he heard something large moving through the bushes, snapping twigs and branches, making audible grunts along the way. Scared of the noise, the pasty teenager hid behind a large stump, fearing the arrival of a bear or moose. Then, to his surprise, a dark-skinned boy stumbled out of the bushes and onto the pathway.

And he was naked.

The boy looked about his age, and his dark skin was covered with cuts resulting from his bushwhacking. *I know this boy. I've seen him before. I have to talk with him—he'll know what's going on.* He arose from behind the stump and let the other boy see him.

"Holy shit!" he shouted in surprise and covered his genitals immediately with his hands. "Shit man! I didn't even see you!"

Averting his eyes shamefully, he apologized. He was glad *he* was the one standing behind the stump.

"No, no. It's okay," the new boy said, still covering himself. "But...man, am I glad to see you."

"Do...do you know who I am?"

"Sure I do. You're Daniel." The dark-skinned adolescent said, looking uncomfortable.

Daniel. It was as if a light bulb switched on within his brain. All of a sudden he remembered that name. *Daniel. Yes, my name is Daniel.* He looked down at his dirty hands. *Daniel's hands. These are Daniel's hands.* He looked at the other boy again.

"How did you know my name?"

"I don't know. I just knew it," he said. He shivered and looked over his shoulder, as if he sensed that they were being watched.

Watched. As if they were being watched.

"Who are you?" Daniel demanded.

The boy turned back to him and eyed Daniel suspiciously: "You don't know me?"

"I don't remember anything."

"That's weird."

"I know. What's your name?"

"Mike."

Daniel opened his mouth to ask more questions, but Mike seemed to be disinterested. He was looking behind him again, along the deer path, towards the direction Daniel had been moving. Finally, Mike turned from him entirely and continued to stare down the path. *As if they were being watched.*

"What's down there, Mike? Do you know what's down there?"

Mike turned back and gave him a blank stare. "I have no idea."

The deer path stretched and twisted beyond their view. There was something odd about that deer path, something that neither Daniel nor Mike could explain. It was almost as if an unusual magnetic force was pulling them down the path and into oblivion. *Pulling them. Watching them. Needing them.*

"Well then, I guess we better keep moving." Daniel moved from behind the stump, no longer caring about his indecent exposure. Mike seemed to feel the same way, and they both began to walk down the deer path.

They moved in silence for a while, absorbing nature around them. Powerful winds swirled through the gnarled trees, carving pathways for the airborne leaves and pine needles that assaulted their bodies frequently. The temperature was dropping and the sky was getting darker. *Need to reach the end; the end of the path.*

Finally Mike spoke, "What do you think has happened to us?"

"I have no idea."

"Do you know anything?"

"I know we're in Canada somewhere," Daniel said as he looked at Mike's face. His face remained expressionless.

"What?"

"Nothing," Daniel turned away. There was a pause, then he turned back to Mike and asked, "Is that blood under your nose?"

"I have blood all over my body."

"I see that, but I mean—was your nose bleeding earlier?"

"Yeah."

"Mine was too," Daniel uttered.

Mike examined his nose and shuddered. "Some weird shit's goin' down, man."

"I know."

"Look," Mike said sharply, gesturing to the right of the path.

It took a few moments for Daniel to find what Mike was gesturing towards, but eventually he caught a glimpse of something through the bushes. It was something bright orange, like a hunter's tent or jacket. Peeking just slightly over a rocky ridge, Daniel could see that there was a little path leading to it from the deer path.

Daniel was excited to see what it was, but he didn't feel drawn to it like he did the deer path. Mike was the first to move toward the ridge.

"C'mon," he said, stepping over a fallen log. "I hear voices."

"But what about the path?"

"We'll get to that later."

Daniel was reluctant to go.

As they ventured over the hill they discovered, to their delight, voices and smells of food, something that the both of them had been yearning. The orange object turned out to be a pitched tent, and across from it, another tent lay fitted for use. In the middle of the tents, there was a fire ablaze, with two people sitting at its side. This was a sight for sore eyes, and Daniel was eager to announce his arrival. Deep in his heart, he knew that he was connected to these people sitting by the fire. Mike too. *Somehow...I know them all.*

The reaction of the two boys was not what Daniel had expected it to be. They twisted their clothed bodies towards them and waved, almost as if Mike and he were expected. One of the boys stood and grabbed blankets from inside the tent.

"We knew someone else would come," the boy said as Daniel and Mike descended from the top of the ridge. He handed out the blankets. "Come sit by the fire, you must be freezing."

They did, and to their own great surprise, they discovered that these boys were in the same position they were: lost. Carl and

Alex were their names, and they did not hesitate at all to share all their things with them. They fed him and Mike, and also gave them warm clothes to wear. Minutes later, they found themselves all sitting around the fire and talking about the situation they were in.

"We're all friends, all of us," Carl told them. "Alex and I found this place about an hour ago; there was nobody here."

"But all the stuff in the tents—it's all our stuff," Alex agreed. He reached into his jacket pocket and pulled out a piece of paper. "This piece of paper—it's a list. It says our names at the tops and then a list of constellations we were looking for."

"Constellations?" Daniel leaned forward. *Constellations.*

"Yeah. Like stars, shit like that."

Constellations. Stars. Daniel felt sick. He didn't like those words at all. *Constellations, Stars.* Watched. As if they were being watched. Bloody noses.

He had to get away. Daniel excused himself from the fire and walked out to the ridge. He could see the deer path below. The trees creaked as they swayed against the frigid wind. It brushed against his face, and he breathed it in like it was God's breath filling his lungs. Night was coming. *It* was coming.

There was something below the surface of this all, but he couldn't place it. *I don't understand. Tell me what's below the surface.*

A new attribute seemed to take on the forest beyond him. As he stood there motionless, the gusting leaves fell to the ground and sat still. The wind that brushed across his face slowed to a halt. *Jesus.*

The veil was covering the forest again. The pressure that he had felt before was coming back, and quickly. He could feel it pressing on his sides—stealing his space and precious humanity.

No!

Daniel did not take his eyes off the deer path. It twisted and moved. *Alive!*

All at once, Daniel leapt forward, all while tasting the fresh blood that oozed from his nostrils and dripped off his chin. He dashed down the ridge and through the bushes, not concerned about the branches that cut through his clothes. He felt no pain.

He stepped onto the deer path and ran as fast as he could, but the unknown pressure was too strong, and his movement slowed to a snail's pace.

Daniel's world liquefied at that moment, along with his joints, his sense of touch, and his hearing. All that was left in front of him was a melting pathway—unreachable, *unthinkable*. The forest was no longer a forest; it was a series of colours and shades depicting a futile direction of light: brown; orange; green.

And at that moment of emotionless ecstasy, Daniel remembered.

Everything.

To Kill a Cat

Robert Burgess Garbutt

The cat delicately raked its moist paw across its ear twice, then applied its pink tongue again. Michael watched with disgust. He loathed the cat. He detested every inch of its soft, creamy body, its chocolate ballet dancer's legs, its dark velvet ears and long curling tail. He wished it gone from his life. And, more to the point, from their lives.

"She loves that furry freak more than she does me," he told Eddie.

"Bullshit," said Eddie, with all the certainty that three Blues could impart.

"I'm telling you. If the house was on fire and she could only save one of us, she wouldn't hesitate a second. She'd save her goddamned cat."

"You're crazy, man. You're jealous over a friggin' cat."

"Damn right. Y'know what? If it was another guy, it would be different. I mean, that I could deal with. I could do something about that. But a cat! What you going to do about a goddamned cat?"

Eddie sipped his beer and considered. "Get rid of it, man. You think about it. How's it so diff'rent from a guy? If it's a guy—what? You tell him to take a hike or you sock him in the eye. Right? So what's so diff'rent with a friggin' animal, when you come down to it?"

"Oh, right! Sure! I punch Ares in the eye and tell him to take a hike!"

"What the hell's Ares? How'd that get in there?"

"Ares is her cat's name. I've told you that." Michael frowned. He sometimes wondered if Eddie really took in anything he was told. The trouble was that, while the guy was seldom really pickled, he was always a little under the influence. It was a miracle he held down his job with Customs, although its being the civil service, Michael suspected you could get away with just about anything.

"Ar–*ease*? What kind of name is that for a friggin' cat?"

"You're getting off the point, Ed. The point is you can't get rid of a cat. They always find their way back. You can drive 'em way out in the country, dump 'em in the middle of a wood and a couple of days later they show up again. They always find their way home again. Surely you heard that song, "The Cat Came Back" when you were a kid? And don't think that cat wouldn't find some way of letting her know what I'd done."

Eddie leaned back against the top step of his porch. "Well, I know what I'd do then…if it was me."

"What?"

"I'd make friggin' sure it never came back. I'd do it in."

"You mean kill it?"

"Yeah. Why not?" Eddie choked on his cigarette for a while. "It's just a cat. It's driving you nuts. You're always on about the friggin' thing. So, do yourself a favour."

"Nah. I can't kill it." Michael scratched thoughtfully at his scrubby beard, then shook his head. The cat might be a king-size pain in the rear and for sure it was screwing up his relationship with Gwen, but she loved it. It meant everything to her. He couldn't just *murder* it. Could he?

"How would you do it, anyway? Run it over with the car?"

"My grandpa, he used to shoot 'em."

"Cats?"

"He hated cats. Like you. Said they dug up his garden. So he'd sit there on his porch with his rifle across his knees and if one came on his property he'd blast away at it."

"Did he ever hit one?"

Eddie slid his glasses halfway down his knobby nose, aware that it lent him an aura of intelligence. At least, that was what Gwen had told him in one of their prickly exchanges, although he sometimes suspected that sarcasm might have been her intention. "The old bugger claimed he killed a couple. You couldn't believe a friggin' word he said. I got a .22 you could borrow."

"Your grandpa did that back in the forties or fifties, when you could get away with crap like that. No way now. The animal rights people would have you in court before you knew what was happening if you tried that today."

I should have taken that .22, you miserable beast, Michael thought, as he watched Ares clean himself. His hand moved stealthily towards his slipper that lay on the floor. The cat paused warily in its task, paw hovering before its gravelly pink tongue. Michael grasped the slipper and raised it nonchalantly, as though reaching back to scratch his neck. The cat's blue eyes flickered towards him. He hurled the slipper and it slashed harmlessly through the space which the cat had occupied a second earlier. Michael cursed as Ares, with a last mocking glance in his direction, sidled through the doorway.

He had barely opened his briefcase when Gwen entered with her careful, dancer's walk, which he had found so attractive when they first met, but which now served as a distasteful reminder of Ares' mincing tread. That same Ares who now lounged innocently in her arms.

"Have you been fighting with Ares again?" she grinned. "Tell me you didn't throw your slipper at him. Will you ever grow up?" She reached for the offending article, which lay accusingly beside the couch.

Michael flushed with guilt. "He was—"

"I do wish you two would get along."

Which was precisely the problem, thought Michael. She wouldn't marry him because he and her cat couldn't live in harmony. That line she fed him each time he pressed the subject, about his being "too immature to sustain a lasting relationship" and her being happy with the way things were for now, it was just a screen. She needed him to love her cat. Scratching under the cat's chin, Gwen pointed to the manuscript Michael had taken from his briefcase. "Have you got something for me there?"

Although she knew he did not edit children's or educational books, it was months since anyone had given her an illustration assignment and she was getting desperate. Recently she had acquired a kiln and taken up pottery as a sideline. She was not yet very skilled, but she had left a few pieces at a friend's gift shop on consignment. Michael had quickly discovered he disliked coming home from work to find her hands and arms bathed in clay. But when he had snidely mentioned that he had never found that girl in "Ghost" the least bit sexy, she had accused him of being unsupportive.

Well, he couldn't support her as an illustrator either, Michael told himself. "No, it's a new novel Tony wants me to read tonight. I've told you, Gwen—talk to Joey Fishe. She's the Art Director. I think there's a new reader coming up."

"Joey Fishe doesn't like me," Gwen sniffed.

"*You* don't like Joey Fishe," he corrected. "Well, if you won't try—" And he turned his attention to the manuscript on which he had to report next morning, but he could not concentrate. His thoughts kept slipping back to Ares.

The cat had hated him right from the start. The first time Gwen had taken him back to her apartment, it had recognized him as a usurper. It had sat on the end of the bed, watching him with its beady, blue eyes, daring him to trespass. And, when he had finished undressing and was sitting on the bed watching Gwen flit about the room, it had peed. Right there on the bed.

"Oh, my God! He never did that before!" Gwen had exclaimed, half in exasperation, half concerned the cat might be ill.

"He hates me," Michael had joked, trying to make the best of the situation, despite the smell, the wet bedspread and his wilted member, which had never fully recovered until the following morning, when Ares had been safely banished to the outdoors.

It had proved no joking matter, for while Ares had never urinated on the bed again, he had gone out of his way to make Michael feel unwanted. Like any doting owner, Gwen had managed to remain blissfully unaware of her cat's tactics. When she looked at Ares she saw only a soft, cuddly creature who loved her. Michael, on the other hand, detected a Satanic cast to the cocky prick of those chocolate ears and the cool mockery in the blue eyes, so like the fiendish feline on the dust jacket of Bulgakov's *The Master And Margarita*.

Although they had never discussed it, Michael could not help but suspect the cat's enmity as the principal reason Gwen would not agree to marry him. Okay, he could admit to being lazy, impractical and a tiny bit overweight and it was true his job paid peanuts, but a few little defects wouldn't bother Gwen. And he didn't accept her spiel that if they "someday" got around to the children she supposedly wanted, she would require someone mature and responsible for their father.

"Once we have the kids, I'd improve," he assured her. "Why shouldn't we make the most of our freedom now—while we've got it? Later, when you have the kids, I'll warm bottles and change diapers and the whole nine yards. You'll see."

Gwen smoothed down the short, dark hair framing her heart-shaped face in a way that increasingly reminded him of Ares' ablutions. "If you look on marriage as some kind of prison," she reasoned in that prissy English accent she clung to, even though she had lived more than ten years in Canada, "I can't see why you're so eager to get into it."

Michael was bewildered. "Prison? What are you talking about?"

"You said you wanted to make the most of your freedom while you had it. I'm saying, if your precious freedom means so much to you, why are you so anxious to give it up?"

"You're twisting everything around," he protested. *The way you always do,* he thought.

There were plenty of times when Gwen really irritated him,

but it did not change his wanting to marry her, prissy English accent and all. He could not imagine ever finding another woman so right for him. They liked the same movies, the same music, the same books; even their careers were compatible—he a junior editor with a publishing house, she a frequently unemployed illustrator of children's books. But, but, but...although they had been living together for nearly two years, he always had the nagging feeling that she might leave him at any time, whereas if they were married she was less likely to walk out on him.

"You're nuts," Eddie told him. "Don't you know half of all friggin' marriages end in the courts these days—what with no-fault divorce and all. Why'd you think a friggin' bit of paper's going to make you safe?"

"I don't know. I'd just feel better. Besides, everyone's expecting us to get married. My parents, my sister, even my boss—all of them keep asking when we're going to get married. After all, it's the next step, isn't it? You go together for a while, then you get married."

"So...What? You believe marriage is forever, do you?" Eddie sounded somewhat incredulous that anyone should be so naïve.

"Well, no, I know it's not," Michael said, doubtfully. "But still... it's more forever than just living together, don't you think?"

"I think it kind of depends what she thinks."

"You've been married—what—thirteen years, Ed? Why did it work for you? Come to that, how did you get Meg to agree?"

"Never had any trouble," Eddie smirked. "She wanted to marry me."

Michael took a look at his neighbour. Reddish eyes behind his thick glasses, two-day stubble on his chin, ragged white tee-shirt barely covering his pot belly and probably his third or fourth beer in his hand. "Can't think why," he muttered.

Eddie raised his bottle cheerfully. "Some got it, some don't."

Michael returned to his own problem. "She says we're fine the way we are for now. I'm too irresponsible. If she thinks I'm so irresponsible, why does she keep living with me?'

"You got a good thing going, buddy," Eddie told him. "Just go with it."

Michael shook his head. "No, there's something else. It's that damned cat bugging her. If it weren't for that cat..."

"Why don't you use poison?" Eddie suggested, when he saw his offer of the rifle was not going to be accepted. "A few pellets of rat poison in the old Whiskas—he'll never know what friggin' hit him."

"For God's sake, Ed," Michael grimaced, "he'd crawl off and die in agony. Most likely right under our bed for effect."

"The trouble with you," Ed grumbled, "is that you're personalizing this."

"It is personal. I don't hate cats in general. I can look at a calendar of kittens without throwing up. I can enjoy a Garfield cartoon with the next guy. I just hate this particular cat."

* * *

"I don't think you've got the friggin' balls for this particular job," an exasperated Eddie had told him. "I think I'm going to have to do it for you, man."

They had mulled over the killing of the cat all summer and Michael had recently noticed that Eddie was losing patience with his pet peeve. His sympathy was now directly related to his lack of sobriety.

So when Michael asked Eddie's son, pimply-faced Mathew, the computer whiz kid, "Where's your Dad?" and the boy said he had gone out with his rifle, there was some excuse for Michael's turning pale and weak at the knees.

"Did he say where he was going?"

"Uh-huh. He said something about getting rid of some cat once and for all."

"Jesus H. Christ!" Michael howled.

"I shouldn't worry too much, Mr. Ruprecht," the boy reassured him. "He was pretty pissed, to tell the truth. The state he was in, I don't think he could hit a barn at twenty paces or whatever that saying is."

But Michael was no longer listening. He pounded down the

street, his eyes raking the neighbours' gardens searching for Eddie or the cat—it didn't matter which. There was no sign of either. Beads of sweat formed on his brow and he was not sure if they were caused by the unaccustomed exertion or sheer panic. If Eddie shot Gwen's cat there would be hell to pay. She would never believe he hadn't put Eddie up to it. It would be worse than if he had done away with the beast himself; it would be as though he had hired a hit man.

He reached the main road and looked desperately from side to side, wondering which way to turn. Cars swished by. Suddenly, there was Eddie, red faced and panting, glasses slightly askew, on the other side of the road. Only he could not see the rifle. Eddie wore a long raincoat that flapped around his knees, like the dusters in old western movies. Was he carrying it inside that?

Then there was Ares, mincing out from under a hedge.

"Ares!" Michael yelled with relief.

Which turned out not to be the best course of action. At the sound of the loathed voice, the cat froze in a crouch. He turned its head slightly to see Michael lumbering towards him at a winded trot. Ares watched until Michael was almost upon him, then darted into the road. He halted as a car, coming in the opposite direction, narrowly missed him, but hovered, confused, in the middle of the road.

In horror, Michael watched a large black Buick bearing down on Ares and realized the cat was too bewildered to move. He hurled himself into the road, scooped up his arch-enemy and continued right into the path of a Lexus in the northbound lane. The impact lifted him off his feet and tossed him, like a bale of hay, into the gutter. Just before his shoulder struck the pavement, he felt Ares' claws dig into his chest as the cat used him to springboard to the safety of the sidewalk.

In the hospital, Michael the hero graciously admired the lopsided vase Gwen brought him as a get-well gift. He did not doubt that she had put much care into its making.

She looked down on him with what he took to be tenderness, and when she muttered, "You silly fool," he knew this was just an expression of her gratitude for his heroism.

Although having one's leg in traction and one arm in a cast was scarcely the most romantic of situations, Michael could think of no better occasion to ask her again to marry him and have her agree. This was his moment. So he asked.

Gwen's eyebrows shot up. "You've got to be joking!" she exclaimed incredulously. Then, seeing he wasn't, she went on, "Aren't I always telling you how irresponsible you are? Why would you seriously imagine I'd marry a silly bugger who'd risk his life throwing himself under a car to save a damn cat?"

A Crescent Moon

Neal Arbic

A crescent moon hung above the Japanese temple in the misty dusk. The ancient stone sanctuary perched high on a dark cliff overlooking the endless sea to the north and a long sloping road down to a fishing village to the south.

That is how Kuroshio village looked a thousand years ago.

Three monks inhabited the stone shrine built in homage to Buddha. The oldest, Hura, a mysterious elder, was said to be able to predict the future. He could barely walk, yet there were stories that on moonless nights he could be seen flying through the air. The youngest monk, Yuu, was no more than twelve years old, very calm and helpful to all. But most popular was Jin, a handsome monk, learned and well respected considering he was only twenty-three. His mother had died in childbirth and, like young Yuu, he was taken in by the kindly old Hura who saved the boys from becoming street orphans.

Every Saturday evening the village made a candlelit pilgrimage to the stone steps their ancestors had built, bringing offerings to the Buddha, money for the monks and flowers for the shrine.

Among the incense and candles, the elders prayed and the children played. Young Yuu enjoyed the company of boys his age and would tactfully lead them outside the temple for games on the grounds. Old Hura sat solemnly leading the chanted prayers to the Buddha for the liberation of all living beings.

And beside him sat Jin, trying his best not to get angry.

Jin was a good monk, however he had one fault: little tolerance for the villagers' children, especially the toddlers who would run around and bang the gong at the back of the temple.

The bronze gong sparkled beautifully in the candlelight and a light touch of the black mallet sent a deep soothing sound throughout the temple and into the night. Its soft ring brought one's mind to rest on its sweet, singular tone. But the children struck it with their fingers, stones and sometimes the hard handle of the mallet in sharp, rapid, annoying tattoos.

Behind his long white beard and bushy white brows, old Hura chanted, unperturbed by the commotion. In private, he scolded Jin for his intolerance and encouraged him to have compassion for others. He pointed out that sooner or later a parent would rescue the gong from over-active hands. And that this was a perfect lesson Jin should take to heart: all things must pass.

Jin was smart enough to know this was good advice, but despite his many vows of patience, come Saturday he sat beside old Hura frowning most miserably.

✻ ✻ ✻

Kei was the beauty of Kuroshio village: at 17, her eyes were as dark as the night sea, her skin tanned as the sands on the village shore, her hair long and dark glistened like the wet nets draping from the seaborne boats.

When Kei walked by, boys paused their play, old men silenced their chatter and girls giggled at the foolishness of men.

In the spring only Kei knew her secret, but by summer her family noticed her changing form when she dressed; by fall the whole village could see she was with child.

She refused to reveal the father.

At last, on a winter night after the child's birth, Kei's father interrogated her relentlessly. Finally, infuriated and broken, she screamed, "I will tell you who the father is! It is Jin—the monk!"

Their small snow-covered hut fell silent.

Ragged, dark clouds passed over a full moon. The temple's windows were full of light. Inside the whole town was chanting and praying. On the long, snaking path up the cliff a lone figure holding a swaddled child approached the summit.

He marched past the village boys playing in the snow. He stomped up the temple's icy steps. Into the flickering light of the shrine stepped Kei's father. Underneath his grey brow old Hura looked up as if he had been expecting a visitor. The father took measured steps toward Jin, who sat beside the old master. As he passed the townspeople, their chanting ceased and their eyes followed him. The temple fell completely silent. The father held out the child to Jin. "Here! My daughter has confessed. Take the child. It is yours!"

The villagers gasped. Jin's mouth fell open. His eyes flashed with anger. Old Hura leaned forward. Jin paused before the old master's stern stare. Jin's shoulders dropped. He lifted his arms to receive the baby and said, "Is that so?"

* * *

The following week young Yuu walked along the shore picking up black pebbles and carried them back to the temple. The fishermen watched him from their boats. The children on the shoreline duly reported the monk's activities to their parents.

The next week Yuu picked up only white pebbles.

No one knew what this meant and it seemed no one would for a while. For on the Sunday after the shocking event, the townspeople still could not believe what had happened. But by Monday most everyone was furious with Jin and ashamed of Kei. By Wednesday discussion began on what should be done. Only on Friday was it finally decided not to visit the temple for a while. Though the villagers agreed this would be best, when Saturday came there was general agreement that their conclusion, though correct, was a depressing one.

On the cliff, under the great eaves of the temple, all was silent. Yuu came and went depositing pebbles into two great piles: one white, the other black. As for old Hura, he spoke to no one except to ask Yuu to collect the different coloured pebbles, and, when Jin tried to explain, Hura stopped him. "Jin, this is your karma—for being so intolerant of children. The Buddhas have blessed you with this lesson. You were right to accept it without protest. Now do your duty. Take care of the child until the Buddhas decide otherwise."

The old master smiled and gently touched Jin's head.

An old woman came for the first week and schooled Jin on caring for the baby. Awkwardly, Jin did his best and soon spent many sleepless nights and tired days looking after the infant.

Old Hura would find Jin in the temple during the baby's naps resting his head on his meditation cushion—sound asleep; the golden statue of Buddha smiled peacefully at the sleeping monk.

Old Hura whispered to himself, "Just as I thought." Gently kicking him, the master woke Jin. "Now you have no time and energy to think about how superior you are to others." The old man laughed. "Come!"

Hura led Jin out into the courtyard and stood between two piles of pebbles, one white, the other black. "This is your new practice, O tired young monk. Sit between these two piles and meditate in the bright sun, it will keep you awake.

"When you have a negative thought, place a black pebble in front of you. When you have a positive thought place a white pebble before you. Everyday make two new piles of stones. They will reveal the contents of your mind on that day. Hopefully, it will inspire you to purify your negativity."

He motioned Jin to sit. "Start now. Do it for one hour."

The old man walked back into the temple and watched over the infant boy while Jin practiced. When an hour passed, Jin arose. The baby had awakened and Hura was feeding him. Jin dutifully took over for the old master.

Old Hura glanced out the window to see Jin's pebbles. Jin had made only one pile of stones—all black.

✳ ✳ ✳

In the first year people were surprised that Jin had not been sent away from the temple. They thought the master too kind. But given time to reflect, most came to the conclusion that Hura was only making sure the baby was looked after properly and that Jin faced his responsibilities. Slowly, people began to visit the temple again.

Jin struggled with taking care of the infant. When he made his daily pile of pebbles there were always more black stones than white, and he would scold himself in a weary voice, "You, Jin, are no monk!"

One day he made a larger pile of black stones than usual. He wept silently before it.

The following winter, people did not think so much about the matter. Saturdays the temple was full of villagers chanting while the young boys played by the temple's steps. People enjoyed seeing the baby grow and begin to walk. Much to Jin's dislike, the little boy was now the most audible culprit in banging on the gong during prayers. Jin could be seen frowning most miserably at this turn of events, yet people generally agreed Jin was a good—though disreputable—father.

Master Hura was pleased. Jin and the little boy became the best of friends. The white piles of pebble were gaining on the black. That summer, under the courtyard's giant weeping willow, Jin could be seen putting the small child on his shoulders and running through the soft draping leaves. The baby laughed and demanded, "Again! Again!"

Jin's love for the little boy grew. By the end of that summer the white piles of pebbles were always larger than the black and he could be heard in the courtyard congratulating himself. "O what a good monk! Surely enlightenment is near!"

* * *

No one had seen beautiful Kei for two years; she became a legend, a myth slipping into the mists of memory. But as summer came to an end, she appeared in the village again. At first, no one recognized her, "Could that be Kei? She looks so old, so grieved."

The sunlight that once emanated from her had been extinguished. People had felt indignant that she had seemingly escaped both punishment and responsibility, but now, on seeing her, they felt only pity.

It was a warm autumn day under the orange sun and the coloured leaves of the temple's garden. The little boy ran laughing as Yuu chased him. Jin sat under the weeping willow delighted with their game. Old Hura usually meditated at this hour, but today he sat on the steps of the temple keeping an eye on the path.

Slowly Old Hura stood up from the step, staring. Jin turned his head and saw them. Standing under the golden leaves of the fall trees were four people. He recognized Kei's father first, then her mother. Jin stood up and saw Kei holding hands with a teenage boy, Mugen.

The father approached as the other three looked on. Upset, almost crying, Kei's father fell on his knees. Overcome with emotion, he prostrated to the young monk and blurted, "Please forgive me, please."

Jin's reaction was fear. Obviously something terrible had happened. He quickly helped the old man to his feet. "Please, what is the matter?"

Through watery eyes, Kei's father explained, "She has confessed. Mugen—" he pointed to the teenage boy holding Kei's hand, "is the child's real father. In fear she named you." Choking on his words, the old man could no longer speak.

Jin looked up from the weeping man and saw Old Hura standing beside him. Hura called Yuu to bring the little boy to Jin. Kei's mother approached and said, "Kei and Mugen are to be married. We are so sorry for all the trouble. We wish the child returned to his real father and mother."

Kei came and stood by her mother. The small child brought by Yuu jumped into Jin's familiar arms, laughing. Kei held out her arms for the child; looking into Jin's eyes she softly said, "You are not the father."

Jin's jaw dropped and his arms tightened around the child. Old Hura cleared his throat and stared sternly at Jin.

Jin bowed his head to his master and humbly handed Kei her child, saying softly, "Is that so?"

* * *

That night the moon was hidden, so the stars shone bright above the temple. Old Hura and young Yuu slept soundly. The village was dark except for a few lights, yet not a sound could be heard. In the courtyard of the temple Jin sat weeping and wailing, piling black pebble after black pebble. But the loudest most heart-wrenching wail came when he lifted one white pebble and placed it on the ground. His trembling fingers refused to release it, and he wept uncontrollably.

* * *

Fifty years later, in the misty dusk, a crescent moon rose above the Japanese temple. Making his way up the snaking path to the ancient stone sanctuary was the now elderly Jin. He had been away for over forty years building orphanages along Japan's coastline. Thousands of young children were now alive, learned and fed because of him. But Jin's spirit was waning and he knew it would not be long before he joined his master Hura in the great beyond.

Yuu was now the temple's old gray haired master. Surrounded by young monks, he bowed to the elderly Jin. Since it was Saturday Yuu gave Jin the place of honour during prayers. He had no idea that night would be Jin's last.

During the ceremony the candles were lit and the incense curled. Amid the prayers and chanting the children ran about laughing and hitting the gong with their fingers and stones. Jin dropped his head amidst the ruckus and trembled. Yuu remembered Jin's dislike for the sharp sounds. He leaned over and asked Jin, "Should I ask the children to stop?"

Jin lifted his head, his cheeks wet with tears. He smiled, his eyes brightly gazing at one small boy about the age of two, who was laughing and banging on the gong the loudest. Jin whispered to Yuu, "No. That sound—is making me very happy."

Kate's Choice

D. L. Narrol

One Friday evening around 8:00, I was purposely keeping my candy stand open longer than usual because I still hadn't seen Sean that week. Just as I started to give up and pack up my stand, I noticed the cargo crew in the distance with a taller man walking with them. That was definitely Sean. He approached me.

"Hello Kate. Yer lookin' rather lovely today," he said bent forward tipping his cap toward me.

I must have blushed because I wasn't used to boys my age ever saying such kind words. He definitely wasn't sixteen or even seventeen or eighteen for that matter. He was a full-grown man. He wasn't as scruffy-looking as the rest of the cargo crew. He was excruciatingly handsome.

I watched him take a chocolate bar and then dump some change on my counter top. "Kate, I see yer just leavin', would ye be interested in havin' a pint with me?"

"Alcohol? No! I don't do that!" I blurted in an overreacted state.

"How 'bout a walk 'round the boardwalk then?" he asked, looking sweaty and tired.

I felt my blood rush to my head. This was a frightening proposition. "Oh, I don't think I can do that!" What was wrong with me? I wanted so badly to be with him. Things were so much more liberated in 1910, where a girl could be on a gent's arm for a short stroll along the boardwalk.

He smiled with a slight chuckle. "Surely ye can."

I was so nervous, I wiped my palms on my skirt. I couldn't take my eyes off of him. His hair was so bright, just as his eyes were bright blue. He helped me pack my stand and then he took my hand. It felt so good to have my hand in his. He led me to the boardwalk. He stopped walking. Then he took my other hand where he brought his body close to mine. My heart almost jumped. He slowly brought his lips to my neck and then the kissing began. I jolted and pulled back. I kept reminding myself he was a man not a kid.

"Sean, where are you from? I know you're not from Toronto."

He paused. "Originally, I'm from County Cork, Ireland. But, I first landed in Ottawa some eight years ago."

"Ireland? That's so far."

"Sure, me and so many others are flockin' to the new world for a better life."

"And you landed in Ottawa. It's our nation's capital you know."

"I know that."

I watched him sigh with fatigue a few times. "Say, what did you do in Ottawa?"

"I worked on the Rideau Canal on a cargo ship."

"Ottawa is so pretty," I tried to keep the conversation going as I noticed the sun set.

"Pretty? It's not pretty when yer workin' on a dirty old cargo ship."

I must admit I felt intimidated by him. "Sean, I really shouldn't be out at night with a man. Do you know how old I am?"

He started to chuckle. "I think you're a beauty that's for sure, but I can't really guess a woman's age."

I must have been blushing at this point where I felt showered by his compliments. "I'm just sixteen."

He kept smiling at me as if he was almost in a trance without giving a response. He slowly moved closer to me, so close I could feel him.

This was my first experience with a real man. I wished he had chatted me up more. "Why did you leave Ottawa?"

"Things got to millin' about with the Shiners."

"The Shiners? Weren't they an Irish gang a long time ago?"

"They had power once, but they's still lingerin."

"I see."

He pressed himself so tightly against me that I felt paralyzed. He moved closer to me moving his lips to mine. I reciprocated his kiss. He was a good kisser. Eventually the moonlight glistened onto Lake Ontario and I was with a real man on the boardwalk. My father would definitely object to me dating an Irish immigrant who used to belong to the Shiners. My father hated the Shiners; he called them hooligans. The kiss was long and wet.

"Sean, it's getting very late. I have to make the last streetcar," I said pulling away from him. "Would you like to walk me to Parliament Street?"

He took my hand and walked me to my stop and waited with me until my streetcar arrived. He was a true gentleman. I've never felt this way about anybody before.

The next morning I had breakfast on the terrace with my parents and little sister. I could barely eat, or even breathe for that matter. All I kept thinking about was Sean. My mother detected something was different about me. My father placed his glasses on his nose and discussed business matters with my mother. He began reading out some of his bank statements. He listed some of his investments and then discussed a cargo ship that he must place a lean on. I choked on my eggs but remained quiet.

"This particular vessel makes its weekly rounds shipping cargo from Quebec and the Maritimes. Unfortunately, the owner is behind in his payments. This ship isn't really doing that well anyway. I see no point in continuing with these people. Bunch of Irish ruffians."

I slowly turned my head toward my father. "I have come to

know the crew of this vessel, father. They're not ruffians at all," I said starting to feel queasy in the stomach.

"Don't speak to these people, Katie! Their immigrants!"

"Father, immigrants are everywhere now. I've taken a liking to them. You do business with Italians all the time."

"I don't have to like them do I?"

I felt completely deflated. I looked at my mother and then my sister. My mother smiled at me. "Father, I don't think you're being fair to these people."

"Katie, something is bothering you?" My mother asked. "Is it a boy?"

"Father, what will happen to this cargo ship?" I asked ignoring my mother's question.

"Well, a lean will be placed on it and the owner will lose the ship."

"What will happen to the crew?" I asked not really wanting to hear the answer.

"Unemployed, I guess. That filthy riff-raff will have to work at the CPR or go back to their country. The CPR seems to hire the lowest type of worker. They're all immigrants there now."

"That cargo ship crew are hard-workers, father."

My father stopped and stared at me. "Why do you have such an interest in these people? What are they to you?"

My mother appeared disinterested in the conversation. She occupied herself with my sister instead.

"I see them at the docks almost everyday where I have my candy stand set up. They're good people."

"They're scum! I demand you move your candy stand somewhere else or you must quit that low life job!"

I could barely swallow. I felt helpless. I slid off my chair and excused myself. I dashed to my room to cry for the next two hours.

That following Monday I didn't look my best but hoped Sean would come by my stand. If I did see Sean this week, it would be the last time. I took a piece of licorice and started to chomp on it like a little kid. I noticed someone standing in the corner of my eye. I looked up and saw Sean standing there. I was startled. He had a black eye and a swollen lip.

"Sean? What happened?" I called out running into his arms.

He stepped away from me. "I was in a fight with someone at the Front Street Tavern."

"Over what?"

"Ye just don't know what its like bein' a foreigner. We're treated like dirt everywhere we go. The English stripped my father's land from him. They did whatever they could to destroy us!"

I felt my entire world crash down upon me. I wanted to cry but I held it in. "Sean, does any of this have to do with the ship you work on?"

"It does. We was in the tavern a few nights ago and my boss disclosed to us that by next week we'll be out of work. We took to some serious drinkin' and started crackin' skulls. Some investor is slappin' a lean on our vessel. Story of my life this is."

I knew he was speaking about my father. "Sean, will I ever see you again?"

His deep blue eyes filled with water and he turned away from me.

"Sean, I really like you. Will we ever be together?"

"I like you too."

I felt weak-kneed and vulnerable. "Sean, I love you." I said it! Now, I did it. I may have scared him away forever. I'm just a kid and he's a man. This must seem like a schoolgirl crush. "I love you." I so stupidly repeated myself.

He stood in front of me and stared at me as he took my hand. He whisked me off to the boardwalk behind a cluster of bushes. It was a hot sticky night. I watched him remove his clothes then he helped me remove mine. We made love until morning.

It was Tuesday, my day off. I hated having days off because I missed Sean so much. My mother noticed me walking a bit different around the house because I was still feeling the pain of my first time with Sean. I suppose I can describe it as a pleasure-pain experience.

"Katie, are you alright?" My mother asked.

"Yes, I'm fine."

"Katie, please tell me if you're involved with a boy?"

I looked at her in the eyes and eased her mind that a boy was not filling my thoughts. I didn't lie to her.

"Katie, help me prepare dinner. Your father will be coming home a little later tonight. He's made arrangements to meet with that cargo crew. He needs to discuss their financial situation with them. I suppose they will soon be without jobs."

I followed my mother to the kitchen. She gave me a bushel of potatoes to peel. "You know, Katie, soon you will be interested in boys. Have you ever thought of this?" My mother placed the potatoes in a pot.

"I'm not interested in boys."

She grinned with delight. "Good, Katie, very good." She pulled out the potato masher and handed it to me. "I hope your father gets in soon. I don't like him spending so much time with immigrants, especially those Irish."

I grit my teeth while immersing myself in the potato mashing. "Mother, I think immigrants are fine people. They're in this country for better opportunities. You shouldn't say such terrible things about them."

My mother began to cackle as if I were the village idiot. It was quite fashionable to detest immigrants I suppose. Suddenly, my father got home. He had a black eye and swollen lip. My mother was horrified as she screamed with mercy.

"Those damn hooligans did this to me! You see! See, Katie, see what these people did to me!" My father shouted as my mother placed an ice pack over his eye.

"The cargo crew did this to you?" I asked almost in disbelief.

"That's right. One of them is particularly hot headed and he punched me with his left hook. Evil man."

I started to tremble. "Which one are you referring to as hot headed?" I asked.

"That tall fellow, Flannery I think his name is. He definitely knows how to fight. He used to be a gang member in Ottawa—he was a Shiner."

"Father, the Shiners don't have the power they used to. They've died out over the years!" I tried to lecture to my father but he never listened to me anyway.

"Scum of the earth! They're absolute scum! The owner actually gave me two payments tonight. They're all paid up but I no longer want to do business with them. So, Flannery slugged me!"

"Sean Flannery hit you after they paid you?" I asked completely horrified.

"I'm going to get the police after him and have him deported. Sean Flannery? How would you know his Christian name?"

I tried to gain control of myself. This was going from bad to worse. I tried to get my father to calm down. "Father, where's the cargo crew now?"

"How should I know? I left them in that musty tavern on Front Street."

I knew I had to see Sean. I smiled at my parents as I edged my way to the door. "I have to go to Queen's Quay. The other girl who runs the candy stand has my cash till for tomorrow. I need to get it from her." I so smoothly lied as I made my way to the door and left.

I stood outside the tavern. I poked myself inside feeling a bit nervous. The tavern was filled with mostly men, tobacco, and alcohol. I peeked in scanning the room for Sean. Sean was sitting with the crew. They appeared a bit rowdy which made me feel misplaced and nervous. Sean noticed me as he staggered his way to me.

"Kate, surprise seein' ye here at the local downtown bar."

"Can we go somewhere to talk?"

"Ye don't want me to buy ye a drink?"

"Sean, somewhere other than here, please," I pleaded.

He took my hand and led me toward the boardwalk again. "Sean, no. We can't do that tonight. We need to talk. Can we go sit in a park or something?"

He kissed me on the cheek. "Whatever suits ye."

We walked to King Street to St. James Park and found a bench to sit on. "Sean, what happened tonight?" I asked trying to hold back my tears. I could smell the stench of alcohol on him. He looked at me and smiled, which emphasized his missing front tooth.

"What ye askin' me? I was mindin' my own damn business when some smug business lord started spewin' his aristocratic bullshit all over me and the crew."

I closed my eyes and began to cry. He took me in his arms. There was something about him that was so dreamy and enchanting. I can't seem to picture him as a gang member. What is my father talking about?

"Ye do love me don't ye?" he said to me as he kissed my neck so warmly.

"Do you love me?" I asked in a calming whimper.

He paused. "I suppose I do," he said taking his time to answer.

"Really? You love me as much as I love you?" I asked boldly.

He nodded *yes*.

"Sean, there's something I must tell you."

"What's that?"

"Sean, that smug aristocratic man in the tavern who almost put a lean on the cargo ship is my father."

Sean stared at me almost in disbelief. "Sakes, what ye sayin' to me?"

"Sean, my father is the investor of the cargo ship. I also love you very much," I placed my hands over my eyes and started to cry like a child.

Sean was motionless as he watched me wail through the park. He was silent while he watched me cry.

One month later, I got up from bed and dashed to the bathroom. I got dressed and helped my mother prepare breakfast.

"Two more weeks before school starts up again, Katie," my mother reminded me.

My hair was uncombed and my clothes just didn't quite fit right. "I don't think I'll be attending school this September."

"Pardon me, Katie? Grade eleven is a very important year."

I slid on my jacket. "I have to go to work now. I don't have time to eat breakfast."

"I really wish you'd quit that silly job. You don't need to work.

Your father and I have told you this."

Later that day, I noticed Sean in the distance with the crew. He walked up to me giving me a nickel for his favourite chocolate bar.

"Kate, don't be so sad. I need to be in New Brunswick now. There's a new cargo company and they need people. I need to go where the jobs are." He kissed me goodbye and wiped my tears.

"Will I ever see you again?"

"If I can help it, we'll soon be together. I'll write ye I will."

He took me in his arms and held me as I continued to cry.

That September my friends were at school, but I wasn't. I just didn't want to attend school. I must have lost interest. I really didn't want to be seen with such children, especially when I had been so intimate last summer with a real man. I was feeling different emotionally and physically.

I helped my parents rake the orange and gold leaves. I took whatever small jobs I could find just so I could continue to make my own money. I felt the climate dampen to a crisp ripe autumn. My friends would come calling for me from time to time but things just weren't the same. I had changed.

I didn't want to be seen with my expanding belly. I really couldn't imagine how I would break the news to my parents, but they would eventually figure it out. Some of my friends guessed that I was expecting but I really didn't say much to them about it.

More time elapsed, still no word from Sean. I would sometimes cry myself to sleep. It seemed like centuries since I last saw him. I watched my mother carefully wrap Christmas garland around the banister while she hummed *Deck the Halls*. Thank God, winter was coming it gave me a good excuse to wear bulky clothes. One Monday afternoon I continued to help my mother clean the house I noticed that my mother looked at me with closer eyes.

"Katie, I really wish you would return to school. It's already December."

I held a basket of freshly ironed linens in my arms. "Mother, I would much rather stay home and keep house with you."

"Katie, are you putting on some weight?"

Oh no, this is it—I thought to myself. "Yes, yes, I am," I turned the other way as I started to march out of the room.

"Katie!" my mother called out. "Katie Armstrong, get back here now! I think it's time you and I have a talk."

I rolled back my eyes as I slowly walked back to her. "Talk?"

She held out a letter to me. "We received this in the post last week. It's addressed to you. It's from a boy."

I leaped to my mother snatching the envelope from her. "From a boy?" I shouted aghast.

"Who's Sean Flannery? This name sounds familiar."

I possessed over the envelope tearing it open and I bolted to my room. "He's nobody, mother!"

As I continued to rip away at the envelope, a train ticket fell to my bedroom floor. I picked it up reading it over where it said Toronto—Moncton. "Moncton? That's in New Brunswick. There was a letter folded very nicely which read:

> *To Kate,*
> *It's taken me some time to get settled here. I've land-*
> *ed a good job with an Atlantic cargo company. I'd*
> *like it if you'd come see me. I sent you the train fare.*
> *There's only one catch, it's a one-way ticket.*
>
> *Love Sean*

I had to sit down. My body tingled. I could barely breathe. The train fare was for that coming Saturday morning. I remained in my room trying to figure out how to pack. When my father got home I joined my family for dinner. My father was quiet as he fixed his eyes on my belly. I sat myself down beside my sister at the table. I watched my mother place portions of shepherd's pie on our plates. I stared at my parents and went over my speech before I dared open my mouth.

"Father, mother—I have something I must say to you," my palms were wet with sweat so I wiped them on my skirt.

My parents stopped what they were doing and gave me their

undivided attention.

"I'm leaving for New Brunswick on Saturday."

"Pardon me, Katie?" my father asked with a raised tone.

"I'm leaving here. I'm leaving this house. I'm leaving Toronto. Saturday morning I will be on a train to Moncton."

My mother looked horrified as she started to quiver then looked at my father. "Katie? Who's the boy?" she asked.

I paused. "No boy. I'm traveling to Moncton to be with a man."

My father looked at my mother. "Good God!" My father shouted as he bent his head over the table. "Who is this man, Katie?" he asked.

I swallowed a few times. "Sean Flannery."

"This is about that letter isn't it? I should have never given it to you," my mother said.

"You did the right thing, mother, thank you. You see I'm having his baby and I need to be with him. He now works in New Brunswick because father chose not to invest in the cargo ship. I hope both of you will help me to Union Station on Saturday. I have some luggage that I'll need help with."

The Church of Auvers-sur-Oise

Kira Dorward

Marie Gachet was not a woman to make small concessions. In whatever she did, she was beyond reproach. She had been born and raised in Auvers-sur-Oise, the valley town beyond the hills of Paris. Upon the hill of the town rested the church. From its vantage point the church surveyed its hamlet of loyal patrons. Within its stonewalls lived a constant watcher; His vigilant eye forever focused, all knowing, His judgement their failings.

And that was where Marie carried herself now, up the path leading from the town to its church, her carriage heavy with Catholic guilt. The steps on the path were deliberately raised high, the extra lift penance for those who were unworthy to make their way to this house of God. Marie pushed the heavy wooden doors of the church open and their creak announced her presence to the empty chapel. The air was weighted with the scent of pine and atonement. She did not have to search; she knew where He would be. Pulling aside the red velvet curtain with her weathered hand, she took her usual seat in confessional.

"Pardonnez-moi, Seigneur, parce que j'ai péché."
Forgive me, Lord, for I have sinned.
"It has been two days since I last confessed."

"Continue, *mon enfant*. Repent and be forgiven."

"The man returned last night, that sinful painter. I begged Paul to keep the door shut against him, leave him to the night where such people belong. He brings his ideas and he possesses *mon cher* with them. They are not right with the church, *seigneur. Quelle péché!* They drink the devil's drink and laugh at sacrilege. Paul expects me to serve Satan's dog. And he is my husband, *mon seigneur.* But in serving him I betray *mon Dieu,* the highest of authorities. And then he tells me he is to be in one of *his* paintings! *Je m'en fiche,* it is too much. What am I to do?"

"It is not for you whom I fear. *Non, mon enfant, l'enfer, c'est pas pour toi.* It is for your husband we must pray. It is for him we must act. He is a good man, but without our guidance he will not be meeting you in the hereafter."

Marie clasped her hand over her mouth as a tear streamed down her anguished face, tracing the sagging line of her chin.

"He falters with this painter, *pas de consequences*."

Marie slowly nodded her head in assent, her eyes shut tightly as she rocked backwards and forwards on the hard wood of the confessional seat. Père Vieilli was revealed as the confessional barrier was raised, his face, usually as blank and lined as a piece of canvas, suddenly animated when faced with the threat of a heathen amongst his flock.

"Something must be done."

* * *

"*Le grand fou* would have me believe you are the devil incarnate, *mon ami.* I was told under no uncertain terms by both him and my wife to never see you again, for the sake of my eternal soul."

"Your eternal soul would be lucky to escape an eternity with your wife's, my good Doctor Gachet," was the painter's reply. His subject chuckled, but the doctor's clever eyes also surveyed the room with a sudden rush of guilt that the painter had seen before, when he had painted the church on the hill and witnessed others, like Marie, on their way to an absolution. Scoffing, the doctor leaned back onto the sofa on which he posed, rather uncomfortably, with his elbow on the table and a good part of his torso suspended between the two. His artist friend assured him that the forced perspective employed was absolutely necessary, and not even the master painter could imagine the visual variables without this lengthy exercise. "Be still, or you will ruin my masterpiece," he reproached with a smile in his eye. "I may not be a theologian *comme* Père Vieilli, but it sounds as if Marie believes she is nearly as qualified to deliver such a judgement as he."

"*Néanmoins*, that explains why we are now forced to paint here," the doctor said indicating the inn's room in which the master was now at work. He looked away from his friend as he said this, his careless tone and look avoiding that steady gaze, well used to seeing what was hidden to others. "I'm afraid you are *persona non grata* at the Gachet house, though not by the word of the master himself."

There was a pause in the conversation. The painter dreamed silently in watercolours and the subject dreamed lazily in the mid summer haze. The heat seemed to have settled about the room like dust; and the very air, in the inn and filtering in from the town, discouraged too much unnecessary movement.

A bumblebee oblivious to this universal mood wandered in through the open window, as the breeze would not, and circled around the portrait subject. Paul Gachet swatted it about and in so doing shattered the established tranquillity of the afternoon. He laughed as he missed it and sent it off course to thump into the back of the canvas. The painter sighed and thinned his lips together in frustration.

"Oh, Vincent, it would not ruin your *chef-d'oeuvre* to hint at having a sense of humour. You are too serious about your painting. Try to enjoy some small part of life."

Vincent seemed to consider his friend for a moment. He raised his prominent brow, his eyebrows a defiant ginger like his hair and the beard which traced the gaunt outline of his face. Gachet met the sad eyes he had come to know so well, that would always keep people at a distance with the respect that such subtle, visual misery commanded.

"*Je suis un artist, Paul,*" he responded, in a way that did not address any direct question, "I paint people and landscapes. What I see and feel already exists, captured by my mind onto a canvas. I can imitate and perhaps enhance life, but if it were not already there I could not create it. I cannot put something into being if I do not have the muse." There was again a stillness about the room, though this one was markedly more uncomfortable than the one before. Gachet shifted slowly from side to side in his position, rocking about in slower intervals, constantly readjusted his arm, and made more audible noises of irritability. The artist, frustrated himself, grew angry and threw down his brush.

"We will finish another day—"

"—My wife, she will be expecting me home."

❊ ❊ ❊

And the painting would be finished, but its subject was never again present. The painter's brushstrokes were now heavy, a labour of duty and not of love—an effort to finish and prove some small measure of his worth. Alone in his room, above the inn's pub, talk and laughter might rise up through the warped and aging floorboards. But when the artist drank, he drank alone.

Dr. Gachet was a busy man. There is no rest for the wicked or the only doctor in a small town. But no longer did he spend his few moments of leisure with an artist in an inn room. Père Vielli, like the good doctor, now made house calls. And Marie, knitting by the fire, always had her mind on prayer and her eyes on her husband.

Months passed before communication was reduced to a meagre note accompanying a covered piece of canvas, without a frame, delivered to the house of the good doctor reading: "To my muse. *Sincèrement, l'artiste du diable.*"

❊ ❊ ❊

"*Dr. Gachet, levez-vous Monsieur*! You are needed in the town."

The messenger ripped the duvet off the portrait sitter. Probably in reply to the look of indignation he justly received, he continued, "There has been...an incident. At the inn. *Allez-y toute de suite!*"

Gachet needed no more prompting from his bed.

With an overcoat too light for the November weather flapping around his knees, Gachet burst into the room that had served as the setting for his portrait. Its painter lay in the bed with a stain of red sheets as his cover. From the evidence lying crimson beneath his feet, the doctor was able to accurately gauge the situation.

"*Mon Dieu mon ami,*" he said running his hand over the forehead glistening with perspiration, "what have you done?"

"*Le fou* staggered through my whole bar in that state," said the obviously uninterested and irritated landlady. She had seen too many incidents come and go through her establishment to be anything else. "Put the other customers off their *patis. Maintenant,* I will not have him getting some strange disease and infecting the whole place. He does it without a fuss, if he dies."

While the proprietress had been loudly voicing her annoyance, the doctor had been assessing his patient.

"It was his own doing, it would appear. Even with my experience, I do not think the bullet can be removed. Too near the artery." As he said this, the shape beneath the crimson stained sheets groaned in sheer wretchedness. "He has probably not much more than a couple of hours. *Envoyez le garçon,*" he nodded at the messenger who had woken him from his sleep, "*à Père Vieilli.* Do not elaborate on the circumstances and I will give you what it is worth in francs."

When Vieilli swept into the room, Bible in hand, and daunting wooden cross, tucked in the folds of his billowing black cloak, the doctor rose from his post beside the bed to his feet. There was a tremor of excitement about the priest now; in presiding over matters of such seriousness he was most aware of his position of power over the realms of the living and dead. No souls from his parish would pass peacefully into the afterlife without his permission.

"*Mon cher Paul,* I am not too late, am I?" As he said this he glanced over at the occupant of the bed, and in an instant thinly veiled disapproval clouded over his face, the apparition of storm clouds visible in his brows. "Really, I would not have expected such from *you*, Doctor Gachet."

"*Mon Père*," Gachet began his entreat, "remember forgiveness and the teachings of *notre Seigneur*. For this too is one of his sheep."

The shuddering, wracking gasps of the artist was then the only sound in the room. The priest considered him a moment. Without another word to the doctor, and still with thin-lipped disapproval, the priest bent over the man lying near death and performed the last rights. Only Gachet and the messenger boy would be witnesses to these final moments of the painter's life, and later the same party would be the only ones to attend the funeral. As Père Vieilli chanted the last of the Latin hymns, the winds of an autumn night, death transcendent in the very season, curled around and swept off the soul of *l'artiste du diable*.

In the Line-up

Michele Green

My fingers flit like spiders across the spines of the novels on the shelves. What book will I choose today? How will I while away my afternoon in the bookstore's over-stuffed leather chairs, engrossed in my favourite pursuit?

No—that is not truthful. Reading is my *second* favourite pursuit. Writing is my favourite pursuit—my passion. Unfortunately I've never written anything—well, anything *good*. I've tapped out a dozen or so mediocre short stories. I've entered a few contests; written the first chapter of three novels. The last chapter of another. The storylines are predictable and lacklustre. My life experience holds precious little to sink my teeth into. I spend hours writing—deleting—writing—deleting—searching for that shining inspiration, the glorious experience that will offer the meaty material I seek.

* * *

I was born in Saskatoon in the early fifties. My sister and I pursued all the traditional middle-class activities—Brownies, piano lessons, church choir. We played outside in the hot, dry prairie summers constructing elaborate tents of blankets slung over the clothesline and held together with clothespins and rocks. We roller-skated. We rode our bikes endlessly through dusty gravel alleys alive with grasshoppers in search of one decent hill that would give us a thrill. We invented plays and choreographed dances and charged our mother a cookie for the pleasure of being our audience. We biked the alleys to the local pool, and biked home again with fingers puckered like pink raisins and toes scratched and bleeding from the pool's rough cement sides.

When I was eleven and my sister was thirteen my parents separated and we moved with my mother to the small town of Moose Jaw. Dad departed for Toronto. It wasn't a messy divorce. They just fell out of love and grew apart—so far apart that my sister and I sometimes felt trapped in the chasm between them. But there was certainly nothing dramatic to write about.

* * *

Today the bookstore is preparing for a book signing—a 'local author' none-the-less. I slip over and grab one of the copies stacked on the signing desk, hoping it is someone I've read. But no—it is the first novel of a man named John Brolyn. The slim volume is titled *The Family Next Door*. I scan the dust jacket's bio. The name is a pseudonym and the author has written the novel while serving a stint in jail. A government-funded literacy improvement program, no less. When I see his picture I recognize him. He hasn't put much effort into disguising his name. I know I'm looking at my childhood neighbour, Jack Dolyn.

Jack was five years older than me. He lived across the alley and several houses away with his mother, a small Hungarian woman who spoke broken English. Jack was always in trouble for something or other. I remember his mother's voice, "Yackie, Yackie, you get back in dis house right now! Yackie do you hear me?" 'Yackie' never listened to his mother for one second as far as we could tell. She shook her broom threateningly in the doorway as he escaped on his bike and sped off down the alley, gravel shooting in his wake like gunfire. He was a big, muscular kid and could have ripped the broom out of her hand and pummelled her to death in a second if he'd wanted to. We were actually surprised that he never had. Our family had had a few confrontations with Jack Dolyn when we were young...I hadn't thought of him in years.

A line-up is forming in front of the table. An eclectic assortment—some look fresh out of jail themselves, here to support a fellow inmate. A few women in their twenties and early thirties shush the preschool children hanging on their legs. A smattering of nondescript middle-aged men and women swivel their heads back and forth to the front door, anticipating the author's entrance.

The faces in the line-up have one thing in common—they are excited. Genuinely excited. In an unsettling sort of way. They look as if someone is about to air some dirty laundry—to tell all. I've noticed that look on the expectant faces of raunchy TV talk show audiences. I can see the novel peeking from purses and cloth bags or clutched under arms.

"Have you read it yet? Do you think it's more fact than fiction?"

"I know it's a 'novel' but I've heard it's autobiographical."

"The story takes place in Saskatoon. I wonder if it *really* happened here? And who *were* those crazy neighbours?"

The talk is an unnerving buzz. If there *is* any truth to the story about the 'family next door' maybe I'll recognize them. I slink behind a panel of books and settle into a chair within earshot of the expanding line-up.

The novel was written in the first person in the voice of a young girl, Audrey. Her older brother, Jack, bore a striking similarity to the real Jack. Jack did not have a younger sister—or an older sister—he was an only child. Fiction, I acknowledge, with a tinge of relief, definitely fiction.

I am about to start a quick perusal when a woman's laugh distracts me.

"It's sick, really, but have you read the bit where the father from next door breaks into the house while they're on vacation and wanders around the house with little Audrey's panties over his head and her training bra stretched over his big chest? It's perverted...but it's a funny picture to imagine."

The book slips out of my hand and falls to the floor.

* * *

Jack wasn't talking about some imaginary neighbour's family—he was talking about *my* family. But it hadn't been my father who broke into his house; it was Jack who broke in through our bathroom window. And it was *my* underwear and training bra that he pranced around in—with all the lights on, no less. The neighbours knew we were away for the night and phoned the police. Jack was charged with break and enter but he was under sixteen and was home lounging in his backyard the next day. We could see him over the hedge and across the alley when we stood on tiptoe on our back steps.

There had been other times, too. Times when my sister and I would open our bedroom drapes and find Jack standing on the fence, his face only inches from the window. He'd jump down and dash away before we could squeal for our parents.

He gave us three little brown frogs one summer day—handed them to us over the gate because we weren't allowed to let him in the yard. We made them a house out of a cardboard box with a plastic container as a pool and a pillow from our dollhouse and put them under the back steps for the night. In the morning they were dead—squashed flatter than pancakes on the landing. We didn't tell our parents; they would have been angry that we had accepted them from Jack in the first place. We scraped them off the pavement and had a funeral in the vegetable garden with Popsicle stick crosses and cardboard headstones. The whole time Jack rode up and down the alley on his bike, ringing the bell in an endless shriek.

Once he grabbed a cat by the tail and swung it in circles over his head until its eyes bled. I can't remember if I actually saw him do it or if I just heard about it. But Jack Dolyn scared the hell out of my sister and me. He scared the hell out of the whole neighbourhood.

* * *

The line-up bursts into applause on the other side of the shelves and I know John Brolyn/Jack Dolyn is making his entrance. Peering between *Canadian Shade Gardening* and *Canadian Woodland Plants* I watch him pump hands with the staff before taking his place behind the table. He is a weathered, balding middle-aged man, years older than the book jacket photograph, but it is him all right. I sink back into the chair and retrieve the novel. The cover is slippery between my perspiring palms.

To the background of "I just loved your book...", "Could you sign it to...?", "How long have you been out of jail?", "Have you started a second novel?" I speed-read my way through the chapters.

> *My bother, Jack, was a handsome, strapping young lad who, at an early age, shouldered the responsibility of male head of the family for our mother and me. Jack was fifteen and I was seven when his job as protector took a crucial turn. I had already experienced first hand our neighbour's secret and had kept a painful silence. It was a relief when Jack began to see behind the false front of the Preston family—the smiling wife, giggling daughters, manicured lawn and neatly trimmed hedges. Jack and I both knew that when Mr. Preston was washing and polishing his car his mind was on other things...*

It was my family all right, but my family seriously twisted. I read on with mounting apprehension.

> *On evenings when Mrs. Preston left for her night shift as a nurse at the local hospital, I could feel Jack's mood change as he read me a bedtime story and tucked me into bed. In the darkness of my room I heard him pacing from window to window, observing behind closed drapes as Mr. Preston left his sleeping daughters and crept out the back door...*

In reality my father was a firefighter who worked shift work many nights, leaving my mother alone with us. My life swam between fiction and reality.

> *Jack followed. Hiding behind trees and around corners, he watched Mr. Preston play peeping tom. He*

watched the man's careful avoidance of homes where
barking dogs might sound the alert. He watched him
jigger window latches...
I screamed Jack's name over and over when I saw the
shadow and felt the draft of the curtains fluttering
at my open window. Jack lurched to my bedside in
time to see the man running through the backyard.
Mr. Preston—we had no doubts...

"John...John, can you tell us...how much of this novel is auto-biographical?"

I stop reading.

"Well," he drawls. "Well...I think most writers write about stuff they know. And what do we know better than our own lives? But hell no...for the most part it's just a story I made up. Goddamn, if any sick bastard had really done those things to my little sister I'd a killed him. Just like Jack did in the book."

My reading speeds up, bouncing over the crudest descriptive sections and becoming more fragmented in an effort to keep ahead of the conversation.

Gentle, caring Jack could no longer stand by and
observe this vile predator...Awaiting Mr. Preston
in the alley, Jack pounces, smashing his brains out
with a rock...

The picture is unsettlingly similar to the episode with our little frogs.

...Jack takes his punishment like a man...lenient
sentence...model prisoner...community hero...

"John, if some of this story is true, did you really marry the pervert's daughter?"

I haven't read that far and my stomach turns at the thought.

"It's fiction, man," Jack says. "It's a made up story. No, I didn't marry the pervert's daughter. I didn't marry nobody."

In the final chapter of the novel Jack is released from the Prince Albert detention centre and looks up the sisters who are now young, voluptuous women eager to repay him in any number of outrageous ways for ridding the world of the scourge that was their father. I can't read the last chapter. I don't want to know which of us was the lucky bride. I hope it was my sister.

I close the book, seething with anger, like a raging bull with a spear embedded deep in its side. That son of a bitch stole the only good story of my childhood. I'd forgotten all about Jack and his antics. I know I could write a much more insightful, realistic portrayal than the comic book/harlequin romance/pornography he has produced.

I move to the end of the line-up. I'll tell him what I think of his disgusting, warped version of the truth. I'll slap him across his wicked, stubbly face.

The line inches forward, another happy customer served. Three people remain in front of me.

I'll tell him I'll sue him for defamation of character. Even though he changed our names and the circumstances, it is obviously my family. Anyone would be able to see that.

Two people.

I'll tell him how *dare* he transform fact into fiction. How *dare* he take my past and use it for his own gratification. How *dare* he...

One person.

How *dare* he...what? He did what I had been unable to do. He had taken his experiences and used them as a basis to create a fictitious world. The past was there for me just as it was there for him. The difference was that he had done something with it and I had not.

"Hey there," Jack says to me as he scrawls 'best wishes, John Brolyn' on the title page, "have you read the book yet?" I bear slim resemblance to my eleven-year-old self and he doesn't recognize me.

"Ya," I mutter. "Ya, good imagination."

"Thanks." He closes the book and slides it across the table.

Biographies

Lindsay Allison is a first year English student at the University of Toronto and has been writing fictional stories since she was four. At fourteen years old the inspiration for The Stones came to her from the many years of gazing at sunsets.

Neal Arbic is a yoga teacher, musician and writer. He is author of Yoga for the Soul. His books and CDs are available through his website: BecomingPeace.net.

Robert Burgess Garbutt is a book designer by trade and author of numerous music-related magazine articles and the book *Rockabilly Queens: The Careers & Recordings of Wanda Jackson, Janis Martin & Brenda Lee.*

Michele Green is a graduate of the Humber School for Writers Creative Writing Program and currently works as a freelance writer. She is a core writer for In The Hills magazine and author of *David Earle, A Choreographic Biography*, published 2007.

Jerry Levy's fiction has appeared in many Canadian literary magazines/anthologies, such as The Nashwaak Review, All Rights Reserved, Inscribed, Ten Stories High, and Steel Bananas Anthology (Gulch). He is currently writing a children's novel and looking for a literary agent.

Peter Muhvic, who aspires for a lot while achieving none of it thus far, frequently fibs to appear worthwhile. He also recently saved a woman's life after she slipped off a cliff by jumping to her rescue and using his own body to break her fall.

D.L. Narrol (Dianne) was born in Toronto and resides in Caledon. Her first novel, *Prehistoric Journey: The First Expeditions* was released June 2009, published by Double Dragon Publishing.

Raisa Austina Palha is currently completing her B.A. at the University of Toronto. Her short stories and poetry centre around themes of feminine identity, spirituality, alienation, and the immigration experience.

Sarah Patterson is a young writer who finds inspiration from the world of nature. She currently lives in Bolton, but during the summer she enjoys spending time in Parry Sound, Ontario.

Stephen Wilsher loves nature and that tends to inspire his writings. He has a strong scientific leaning and taught in the school system for 12 years. Poet-philosopher, Dr. Kenneth George Mills, has been his mentor and greatest inspiration in life.

Kira Wronska Dorward is an undergraduate student at Trinity College in the University of Toronto. With her education she hopes to keep writing. This work is dedicated to Aurélien Stoclin, who was there from the beginning.